## THE NORTHLAND CHRONICLES:
# A STRANGER NORTH

## HENRY J. OLSEN

*For my father*
*The man who helps everyone*
*and asks for nothing in return.*

I'd like to thank the following people for their help in making *A Stranger North* a fun sci-fi adventure.

Charles Borchert
Andrew Browne
Chris Garland
John Maresco
Gary Olsen
Gaila Olsen
Stephen Robak
Stanley Serkosky
Judy Serkosky
Elaine Smith
Claude Smith

*"Lastly, private, if you ever see the man in this photo, you are to report to HQ immediately."*

# Prologue

*Central Ontario, Early Summer, 2036*

"HEY ARISTOTLE," Jackson shouted across the saloon. "Who's Bertrand Russell?"

Without so much as a blink, Aristotle continued to read her book, a hardcover that looked heavy enough to snap a moose's back.

"I told ya," Grant said, elbowing Jackson in the ribs. "The woman is an ice queen. Looks like *you* owe me a drink."

Franco, owner of Franco's Saloon, smirked in amusement from behind the counter. The sun had just fallen below the horizon, yet Jackson and Grant were already heckling the other patrons. This was going to be a long night.

"Wait, let me try one more time," Jackson said. He stood six foot five, with ice-blue eyes and dirty blond hair. Years of farm work had given him enough strength to wrestle a black bear. His body was a weapon all in itself; the pistol at his hip was merely a backup.

"Hey Aristotle," Jackson shouted. "What's your real name, honey?"

Aristotle didn't acknowledge the comment, as she turned to the next page of her book, *A History of Western Philosophy*.

"Looks like you owe me *two* drinks," Grant said. He was a stocky man, about six feet tall with dark hair. Like Jackson, he was a farmer, though his physique didn't show it. He holstered a pistol as well.

"What's your poison?" Franco asked.

"Whiskey, straight up," Grant replied. "Same for you, Jackson?"

"Fine," Jackson said.

"Two glasses," Grant said, making a *V* with his fingers, "of the good stuff."

"Oh, it's *all* good — only the finest moose piss for you boys," Franco said, giving his bar a once-over as he turned to pour the drinks. He had five customers tonight. Jackson and Grant were seated at their usual stools on the long end of the L-shaped counter. Two other patrons sat on the short end, their backs to the entrance, drinking bathtub brew and bickering about who'd bagged the bigger buck. Franco couldn't recall their names as they didn't come in often.

And at a table near the front door Aristotle sat alone, in the same crimson hoodie she'd worn every day since she first stepped into Franco's a month or two back. She was cute, with round eyes, a smooth nose, thin lips, and short brown hair. Young, too — Franco guessed she was twenty or so. Her real name was a mystery — another regular had nicknamed her Aristotle, "cause she reads too many darn books," as he'd explained. Jackson and Grant thought the name was a hoot, too, so it stuck. Franco wondered what her name really was, but as long as she bought and paid for a drink when she came in, he was content to let it go. She didn't say much, letting the mammoth revolver she always placed on her table speak for her.

Besides, Franco knew she just came to his saloon for the light — the unflickering electric rays that beamed down from above. Since the Desolation, most buildings relied on oil or kerosene lanterns, but not Franco's Saloon. Solar panels, recovered from a derelict office building with help from

Jackson and Grant, charged a battery by day to power fluorescent bulbs late into the night. The lights were a unique feature that few bars in Ontario could boast of.

Franco finished filling two whiskey glasses, eyeballing them to make sure they were even, and slid them across the counter. For their help, Franco had offered Jackson and Grant free booze for three months. He wasn't convinced he'd gotten the better end of that bargain.

"Enjoy the drinks, boys," Franco said.

"One shot!" Grant said, raising his glass and clinking it against Jackson's. Then both men downed their whiskey in one gulp. *One shot, indeed,* thought Franco. The phrase had caught on a few years before the Desolation, imported from some far corner of the world.

"Two more," Jackson said, pushing the empty glasses back across the counter.

"Coming right up," Franco chirped, wondering what he'd been drinking when he agreed to give Jackson and Grant bottomless glasses.

As he began refilling the whiskey, the front door creaked open and a new guest stepped in — a man Franco had never seen before. The stranger set his bulky green pack by the door and proceeded to the counter. He was lean, stood about six feet tall, and wore a dark plaid flannel shirt and tattered blue jeans. A vintage revolver was holstered on his hip.

"Make yourself at home," Franco called out.

The stranger gave an easy nod in reply. That's when Franco noticed the beard, hanging from the stranger's chin like a shrub just begging to be pruned. Franco hadn't seen even a mustache in years, not to mention a full, bushy beard. Every grown man he knew kept his face smoother than a sow's nipple. The line between man and nature had blurred over the past decade, leaving the daily shave as one of few ways a man could stand up and proclaim, "I'm civilized, dammit!"

Without a word, the stranger strolled up to the bar and took a seat next to Jackson.

"Nice beard you got there, buddy," Jackson said. "I think my neighbor's goat has one just like it."

Grant's nose flared as he fought the urge to giggle.

"Don't worry — the drinks aren't as bad as the humor," said Franco. "What can I get ya for?"

The stranger looked up at the taller man from the corner of his eye, then back at Franco.

"Whiskey, neat, if you wouldn't mind," he said with an upward nod.

"Sure thing," Franco said. He grabbed another glass and picked up the whiskey bottle he'd left sitting on the counter. It was running low, and though the label read *Jim Beam*, it hadn't held a lick of Kentucky bourbon in years. Despite the wide assortment of bottles along the wall, Franco's Saloon served only two varieties of hard liquor: clear and brown. Not that Franco went out of his way to advertise that fact.

"What's a scrub like you doing, asking for something 'neat'?" Jackson asked.

"Will you give the guy a break?" Franco said as he slid the drink to the stranger.

"Thanks," the stranger said, lifting the glass to his lips to try the whiskey. "Not half bad."

"Where you from, anyway?" Jackson asked.

"Maine," the stranger replied.

"Oh yeah?" Jackson said. "And how'd you end up here?"

*Fair question*, thought Franco. Without any infrastructure left to provide fuel for motorized transportation, a guy couldn't just hop on a Greyhound.

"I walked," the stranger said.

"Right," Jackson said with a nasal snort. "And my buddy here flew in from the moon." He gave Grant a hearty slap on the back, hard enough to make the hefty man grimace.

The stranger shrugged. "Suit yourself," he said as he lifted his glass and closed his eyes, inhaling the alcohol vapors before taking a sip.

Jackson stared at the stranger for a moment then downed his whiskey in one gulp, slamming the empty glass on the counter.

"I'll have a whiskey, *neat*," he said mockingly, shoving the glass toward Franco.

"How about you let me catch up first?" Grant said, discreetly winking at Franco then taking a small sip of whiskey.

"How about, our friend *Frankie* makes me a drink?" Jackson said.

Franco frowned in reply. He didn't appreciate the nickname.

"Sorry," the stranger cut in. "Is my being here a problem?"

"Oh no, sit and stay awhile," Jackson said with an exaggerated smile. "Bless us with your beardedness, as Frankie pours me another drink." He grabbed the whiskey and swirled it around the bottom of the bottle.

"Jackson ..." Grant soothed, putting his hand on the taller man's shoulder. With a grunt, Jackson shrugged it off.

"No, I think it's about time I hit the road," the stranger said as he began to stand up. "How much?" he asked.

"Two bucks," Franco said. The stranger took a two-dollar coin from his pocket and set it on the counter.

"But it's so dark out," Jackson warned derisively. "There could be wolves out there!"

"I think the wolves will make better company," the stranger said with a grim smile.

The room fell silent — so quiet that Franco could hear the faint buzz of the lights overhead.

"*What was that?*" Jackson demanded.

"Oh, I think you heard me just fine," the stranger said, turning to walk away. "Cheers, boys."

Still sitting down, Jackson reached out with his left hand, grabbing the stranger's left shoulder.

"Stay," he growled.

The stranger stopped.

"Let go now," he said, "and I'll call us even."

"That right?" Jackson said, rising from his stool. He towered over the bearded man.

Franco mouthed "No" at the stranger, while making a throat-slash gesture. No one got into a fight with "Stone Fist Jackson" and escaped without a broken bone or two.

A wry smirk stretched across the stranger's face. *Does he know something I don't?* Franco wondered.

"It'd be a shame if you wasted that genuine Kentucky bourbon on a scrub like me," the stranger said. "Wouldn't it?"

Jackson glanced at the bottle in his hand.

"It's all just moose piss anyway," Jackson said. With an angry roar, he swung the bottle over his head, toward the stranger's skull.

Franco cringed, anticipating the sound of shattering glass.

It arrived — just a little later than expected.

The stranger reached back and clasped Jackson's wrist — the one resting on his shoulder. Bending forward, he yanked on Jackson's arm. Then with superhuman strength, the stranger threw Jackson over his head, effortlessly swinging the man's body through the air like a pickax.

A pop sounded as Jackson's shoulder dislocated. He cried out in pain. Then the stranger released Jackson's arm, letting the giant man's body slam against the floor. Shards of glass scattered about as the whiskey bottle exploded from the force of impact.

Franco's eyes shot wide open — *What the Desolation was that?*

The two men on the short end of the counter must've been thinking the same thing — Jackson had landed right at their feet. They glanced at each other, then tossed a few coins on the counter and hightailed it out of Franco's Saloon faster than two deer running from a wildfire.

With a groan, Jackson sat up, slowly getting to his feet. He stumbled around, woozy from his encounter with the floorboards. His left arm hung limp at his side. With his right hand, he reached for the firearm in his holster.

Grant — still seated behind the stranger — dove to the floor.

"I wouldn't recommend that," the stranger warned Jackson.

Jackson ignored the advice. He pulled out his pistol and cracked the air with a wild shot. The bullet whizzed past the stranger, lodging itself in a bear trophy mounted on the wall.

The stranger raised an eyebrow, then without taking his eyes off Jackson he whipped his six-shooter out from its holster, spinning it around his finger as he extended his arm.

Then his thumb cocked the hammer. His finger pulled the trigger. The bullet screamed out. And Jackson's body fell forward, victim of a gunshot wound between the eyes.

Franco stared at the scene. His brain couldn't process what his eyes had just witnessed. He'd seen death strike before, yet never with such speed and surgical precision.

With a whimper, Grant fumbled for his pistol. The stranger spun around and approached the panicking man with deliberate steps. He slid his revolver back into its holster then clenched Grant's shirt collar with both hands.

"Hammersnap!" the stranger shouted, hoisting Grant into the air. "You wanna die, too?"

Sheepishly, Grant shook his head back and forth.

"Good. Have a safe flight," said the stranger. With a growl, he chucked Grant across the room, as though the man weighed only as much as a sack of potatoes. The air in Grant's lungs rushed out in a loud "Oof" as he crashed against the rear wall and fell to the ground.

*Who is this guy?* Franco wondered. The stranger fought like a robot, programmed to neutralize all obstacles. Maybe he was good with a mop, too.

"You gonna help me clean up this mess?" Franco asked.

"I'd love to, but I think we'd be getting a little ahead of ourselves," the stranger replied, raising his hands in the air. His eyes were focused on something behind the counter.

"What're you talking about?" Franco said, sneaking a peek behind himself. All he could see were a bunch of liquor bottles and a mirror.

"Sorry," the stranger called out. "Did I shoot your boyfriend?"

"Hey now," Franco cried out. "Why, I'm straighter than a —"

"*Boyfriend?*" A woman's voice cut in. "Don't be ridiculous."

*Aristotle!* Franco had forgotten about her. She was still sitting at the corner table, the massive revolver having replaced the book in her hands.

"What's a little thing like you doing with a large bore gun like that anyway?" the stranger asked. "The kick must nearly snap your arms off."

Aristotle narrowed her eyes at the stranger.

"You know why you got a gun on your back?" she asked.

"No, but it's not the first time and it won't be the last," the stranger replied.

Aristotle rolled her eyes. "Both those men must outweigh you by fifty pounds. You tossed them around like rag dolls. Explain yourself."

"Every man has his secrets," the stranger said.

"Yeah? Every man also has his price," Aristotle said, cocking her revolver.

"Shoot me now and you'll never find out," the stranger said. "Besides, I was acting in s —"

"Self-defense?" Aristotle finished his sentence. "Say a little farm dog nips at a wolf. If the wolf rips out the dog's throat, is that self-defense?"

The stranger paused, seemingly caught off guard by the question.

*She's said more in the last minute than she has all month!* Franco thought to himself. He had a unique vantage point. The stranger and Aristotle had to look at each other through the mirror; he could see both of their faces directly.

A moment later, the stranger offered a shrug.

"I've never thought about it," he said.

"Then you'd best start thinking about it," Aristotle said. "Cause you obviously got more power than you know what do to with."

"Well, if it's no trouble to you, I'd like to know the name of my judge, jury, and executioner," the stranger requested. If he was afraid of imminent death, his voice didn't show it.

"Oh, I'm not gonna shoot you," Aristotle said. "Killing you'd be a waste of talent."

The stranger didn't reply for a moment, waiting for Aristotle to say more.

"What'd you have in mind?" he finally said.

"I'm putting you on probation," Aristotle answered.

"You some sort of cop?"

"No, but if you break my terms, you're gonna wish I was."

"Terms?" the stranger with disgust. "I don't live by —"

"I don't think you're in any position to bargain," Aristotle cut him off. "Now listen up. I got eyes and ears all over. If I catch wind of you causing trouble, you're liable to find yourself on the wrong end of my revolver again."

"That's it?" the stranger asked, surprised.

"Well, I'd tell you to get cleaned up and make yourself useful, but it ain't my place to play babysitter — you gotta find your own way," Aristotle said. "Now, you'd best march right outta here. Keep your back to me."

Still holding his hands above his head, the stranger cautiously sidestepped toward the exit, maneuvering around Jackson's dead body then coming to the door. After picking up his pack and swinging it onto his back, he put his hand on the doorknob.

"You know, I never caught your name," he said, without turning to make eye contact.

"They call me Aristotle," she replied.

The stranger didn't say anything for a moment, like he was taking it all in. Then he swung the door outward. A gentle wind rustled through the trees outside.

"The name's John," the stranger said. "John Osborne. Look me up sometime." He raised his hand to give Franco a two-fingered salute. Then he disappeared into the darkness.

# Chapter 1

*Near the Minnesota border, a few months later*

"THIS IS THE GENERAL."

"Private Brushnell of Moose Lake outpost speaking, sir. I saw *him*, sir. I saw the man from your photo."

The General didn't answer immediately.

"You're sure? You know there's a good chance he died along with the rest of the world."

"He had a thick beard but, yes, sir. I'm sure it was him."

"A beard, huh? Interesting … Did he see you?"

"No, sir."

"Good. How many are at your outpost?"

"There are two of us, sir."

"And you're absolutely sure it was him?"

The private paused. He was well aware that this moment could make or break his career.

"… I'd stake my life on it, sir."

"Then I need you to trail him. Take the radio you're using now. I'll have another one delivered to Moose Lake soon. Check in with me nightly at 2100 hours. Report to me immediately if the situation changes. Most importantly, remain undetected. Osborne is touchy — one wrong move and we could lose our chance with him."

"Understood, sir."

"What was your name again, son?"

"Brushnell, sir."

"I have faith in you, Private Brushnell. Help me with this and I see a promotion in your future."

"Thank you, sir."

"The General, over and out."

The radio went silent. The private set it down on the outpost's wooden table. He ran his hand through his short, golden blond hair and rested it on the back of his neck. Pensively, he closed his eyes and took a deep breath through his nose, releasing it with a sigh.

His border patrol duty — nothing but glorified cabin-sitting — was over. Finally he had a real mission. He packed quickly and set out immediately, while the trail was still warm.

# Chapter 2

JOHN WAS A grimy, smelly mess of a man. It was late July, when the days were long and the sun seared the skin. His flannel shirt was a vessel for sweat, his jeans a magnet for dirt. No matter how many times he brushed his pants, the brown muck reappeared immediately. His beard was getting long too. If he looked down, he could see it hanging from his chin.

Unfortunately, appearance and odor ranked low on his list of troubles. Two days ago, he'd used his last .45 round, sniping a squirrel out of a spruce tree. The meat was delicious and his stomach wanted more, but he couldn't hunt without bullets. Knife hunting? He'd burn more calories running around and hacking at rodents than their meat could replenish. Getting into a knife fight with a bear or wolf? Crazy talk — he was resourceful, not insane.

Now, say he got the jump on a moose. A bull moose would outweigh him by a factor of five, but at least the massive herbivore wouldn't have fangs or claws. With a knife against a moose, he might stand a chance. The prospect of a hoof kick to the ribs or a sharp antler to the stomach didn't sound so pleasant. *Better than starving in a ditch though,* he thought.

John looked down the endless path. Usually he could scrounge up ammo from villages or abandoned homes. Problem was that since he'd crossed into Minnesota, he hadn't found as much as a backwoods love shack. Just trees. Trees and water. A boundless expanse of woodland and lakes, interspersed with the occasional trail to nowhere. Beautiful country, zero bullets.

At least he was far away from that pompous wannabe cop in Ontario. She couldn't have kept tabs on him this far south. John didn't intend to cause trouble, but he didn't like the thought of someone looking over his shoulder.

John heaved a sigh of exhaustion. Something wasn't right. His training included combat under fasting conditions — he could go without food for a week and still perform at a high level. Yet now he was starving after two days with no meat, despite eating every berry and piece of fruit he could find? It didn't add up.

*What's that?* His eyes spotted a wooden sign in the distance. His feet grudgingly carried him close enough to read it. The sign read, "FRONTIER VIEW — 2 MILES," in faded white letters. *Finally, I'm getting somewhere,* he thought. He could restock his cache of bullets and maybe get a decent meal. Newfound hope made his pack feel lighter and his feet move faster. He kicked up loose gravel as he sped ahead, leaving a dusty haze in his wake.

Within a couple dozen steps, his second wind blew out as fast as it had come in and a hazy fog crept over his brain. He doubled over, resting his hands on his thighs and panting heavily. A coughing spell hit him, each violent cough singeing his throat on the way out. He looked at his feet. Red splotches dotted the gravel — blood.

Shortly, the coughing subsided and mental clarity returned. *What the broken trigger is wrong with me?* he wondered. His body wasn't using his energy reserves properly — something was impeding the process. But why now? He'd been drifting through the wilderness for nearly two years. An empty stomach wasn't novel. Spitting up blood was.

With a groan, he stood up straight and continued ahead. No way he'd collapse on the road with the promise of civilization just minutes ahead.

As John wandered down the path, a creature meandered out from the cover of the forest, about fifteen yards ahead on his right. A moose? A milk cow? No, neither. John stared at the strange animal. A shiver ran down his spine. It had the head of a Holstein, complete with those immense, vacant black eyes — the same eyes he remembered seeing on milk cows in his youth, which always seemed to peer deep into his soul. Yet the beast wasn't a head of cattle. It had heavy antlers, as well as the arched shoulders and rugged body of a moose. It was a big, brown, furry abomination, and it gave John the willies.

His stomach growled — the animal was also fresh meat. He watched as the beast ambled across the road. It stopped and turned to gaze at him, meeting his eyes. John approached the creature with caution, scheming as to how he could take it down. Not with the knife — if he didn't hit a major artery on the first slash, he'd have an angry frankenmoose on his hands. No, he'd use his arm. A quick bash to the head with his left arm could take it down.

He slowly circled toward the creature, narrowing his eyes distrustfully. The beast continued to stare at him unflinchingly. John winced as stale breath rushed into his nostrils. Apparently the frankenmoose had never heard of mouthwash. John drew his head to one side, deeply dipping his left shoulder and then his right as he examined the creature's head. Though the freakish beast gave him goose bumps, it seemed harmless enough.

*Lunch time*, he thought as he drew his left arm back, preparing to deliver a megaton wallop. He curled his fingers into a fist and threw his arm forward.

Before John's arm could make contact, he felt his legs give out. He collapsed forward, the weight of his heavy pack adding to his downward momentum. The beast pulled back its head to avoid contact, and John hit the gravel trail with a sharp thud.

He remained on the ground, watching the beast's long, bony legs as it casually shuffled past him. Then everything went black.

# Chapter 3

EMIKO CREPT through the underbrush cautiously, her brown shoes moving silently over the grass and fallen leaves. She was a huntress, becoming one with the shadows. The sun shimmered through the green foliage overhead, lending her black hair a luminous sheen. Bangs hung just above her thin, dark eyes, and the rest of her unbraided hair extended halfway down her back, clinging to a woven olive green shirt. She wore dark, charcoal colored pants. Given the summer heat, she'd have preferred shorts, but she knew better — thorns and poison ivy weren't kind to unprotected skin.

She employed only two tools in the hunt: the jackknife strapped to her hip, and the Ruger 10/22 rifle slung across her back. The .22 caliber rifle's oak stock rested near her waist and the stainless steel barrel protruded past her shoulder. She intimately understood its weight and bulk, like a third arm extending from her back, and gracefully compensated for it in her movements.

The sounds of the forest surrounded her. A calm morning breeze whistled through the leaves. Birds chirped their songs from the safety of the trees. While her brother Nathan loved listening to the subtle music of nature, Emiko's ears filtered through it. It was white noise, obscuring the sounds that mattered — the rustle of a squirrel's feet in the grass, or the scampering of a rabbit through the undergrowth. *Those* were the sounds she'd trained her ears to pick out from among the murmurs of the woods.

Beneath Emiko's eyes hung two heavy, dark crescents. Though she wasn't far from home, she had stayed out all night, sleeping only for a few hours in a leaf bed amid a cluster of old spruce trees. Not that she'd planned it that way. Tired from a long day of stalking through the woods, Emiko had sat down to take a rest and accidently drifted to sleep. An honest mistake.

Right now her body wanted nothing more than to go home and sleep in a real bed, but that would have to wait a little longer. She wasn't ready to face *him* yet. She could already envision it. Nathan would be sitting in a chair near the door, waiting for her to come home. She would walk in. He would explode at her, trying to fill the role of their father. She would lash back, reminding Nathan that he was her *brother*, not her dad. That he was only *three* years older than she. That he had no right to boss her around.

They'd fight for a while, then one of them would storm out of their small cabin. It would *probably* be her, and she'd *probably* march right back into the wilderness — the same wilderness she was stalking through right now. So why even bother going back home? Emiko intended to put off her return as long as possible.

Emiko shook her head violently, clearing her thoughts. She absolutely *would not* let her brother ruin her little hunting trip. *No way*.

Ahead, she noticed a thinning of the trees — a trail was near. She set out toward it. From there, she'd be able to clearly see the terrain on either side and instantly determine her location. On any of the trails leaving from Frontier View, she knew exactly how many steps it would take to get back to town. It seemed to be fewer steps every month, but that problem wouldn't last long. Already fourteen and slightly tall for her age, she figured her legs didn't have much further to grow. She looked forward to being an adult. In fact, she already felt like one, yet everyone in Frontier View still treated her like a kid.

With a sweep of her arm Emiko shoved a fir branch away from her face, revealing an old road paved with loose gravel ahead. She stepped out from the tree cover and onto the trail, squinting immediately. The unfiltered sunlight was brighter than she'd expected. Lifting an arm to protect her eyes, she examined her surroundings.

About a quarter mile south a creek bank kissed the side of the road — a distinct landmark. When Emiko bushwhacked through the woods surrounding town, she always had a general sense of where she was, but now she was certain: Frontier View was an eighteen-minute walk south.

*I may as well go deal with Nathan*, she thought. *I can't avoid him forever.* Reluctantly, she started down the trail at a casual pace. There was no reason to hurry the inevitable.

The trail extended forward into the distance, bending behind the trees. An object about 200 feet ahead caught Emiko's eye. It was a large green ... pack? She approached carefully, watching for movement.

*No, not just a pack*, she realized. It was a pack on top of a man, who was lying face down on the gravel. Was he asleep? Wounded? Dead? Emiko quickened her pace, driven by curiosity.

The man remained motionless as she hurried toward him. The green pack rested on his back like a turtle shell, and his face was turned to one side.

As she approached, she noticed his thick beard — a rare sight. Everybody in Frontier View made a point of shaving. Even Nathan, who could only grow a whisker or two, shaved nearly every day. It was just ... what men did. Not this guy, apparently.

She squatted by the man's head to take a closer look. Thankfully, he was still breathing; she was in no mood to deal with a corpse. Taking a step off the trail, she snapped a twig from a small tree and turned back to the man.

"Hey, Beard, are you awake?" Emiko poked at the man with her stick. "Anybody there ... Beardy Beard Beeeeeeaaaaaaard?"

The man didn't respond. Emiko poked him again. Nothing.

What could she do? Even without the pack, the man far outweighed her. She'd have to fetch help.

Emiko stared at the man with intrigue. It wasn't every day she discovered a stranger passed out on the road. Maybe when he woke up, he'd have a fresh batch of interesting tales to tell. *Anything* would be better than hearing another of Pierre's stories for the millionth time.

More importantly, now she had an opportunity to evade her brother's wrath. With a bounding first step, she began to skip toward Frontier View.

* * *

Emiko knew exactly where Nathan would be waiting. Their cabin only had two rooms — a small corner bedroom and a large room for everything else. Modest but big enough for two. Well, except for on those frigid winter days when even a polar bear would freeze after a minute outside. Then it meant she couldn't escape her brother. Talk about cabin fever.

Right — her brother. She mentally ran through her assault plan one final time, then fortified her nerves and pried the cabin door open. The hinges creaked as the door swung inward. She stepped inside, taking a moment to hide behind the door before poking her head out from its cover.

Just as she'd expected, her brother Nathan was in the corner opposite the bedroom, sitting in their dad's handmade rocking chair. He wore a white t-shirt and blue jeans. Thick, unkempt black hair jutted from his head in every which way. He'd likely been sitting in the chair all night, anxiously awaiting her return. When he recognized Emiko the anticipation in his eyes faded and he let out a sigh of relief.

The calm didn't last. Within moments, the hint of joy she'd seen in his expression drowned in a flood of anger, boiling in his eyes as he leapt up from his chair.

"Loons over the moon, Emiko!" he said. "Where the hell —"

"There's a man passed out on the road who needs our help! I think he might be dying!" she blurted out as fast as humanly possible.

"What?"

"A man needs our help. He's unconscious — we'll need something to carry him on."

Nathan glowered at her.

"You're serious?" he asked.

"Yes." Emiko nodded, looking her brother straight in the eye to make sure he'd believe her.

"Alright." Nathan's expression softened a bit. "Let's go see if Cynthia's home — I'm sure she'll help. You can explain everything to both of us." He paused, struggling to recreate his stern expression. "But don't think for an instant that I'll forget about last night," he said, starting for the door.

"Of course!" she replied, knowing that Nathan wouldn't be able to muster his anger again — not until she gave him another reason to, at least. Proud of her cunning, she hurried after him out the door.

\* \* \*

An hour of running to and fro later, Nathan found himself in his neighbor Cynthia's cabin, sitting in a hand carved oak chair next to the bearded stranger. The man was lying in bed under a sheet, comatose. Earlier, after Emiko had explained the man's location, a group of four men — including Nathan — had gone out and hastily carried him back to the village.

The man passed air in and out of his lungs in deep, extended breaths, as though he was in the middle of a profound slumber. He didn't smell of alcohol or appear otherwise ill. Nathan could only wonder why he wouldn't wake up.

He hoped Cynthia would have an answer. She'd stepped out to get medical supplies from the Co-op, leaving him to watch the man momentarily. Cynthia was Nathan's next-door neighbor. Her cabin was eerily similar to his — it felt like he was sitting in his own bedroom. His golden tan skin glowed in the sunlight cast through the lone window, just like it would in his own cabin.

The homes in Frontier View had gone up quickly, leaving little time for customized architecture. The people of the then newly settled village worked together, constructing cabins according to family size. Nathan had come with his father and sister, Cynthia had come with her two small children. That had been nearly nine years ago; now only two people lived in Nathan's cabin. As much as he missed his father, he had to wonder how the three of them would have managed in the small cabin as he and Emiko continued to mature.

He sighed, gazing out the lone bedroom window. Life had changed since their father died — changed considerably. Emiko ran wild now, doing whatever she pleased. Their father had commanded her respect and obedience, but try as he might, Nathan couldn't get her to listen. This was what ... the third time she'd stayed out all night?

Nathan still vividly recalled the last time she tried creeping in after dawn. He had exploded, yelling and screaming at her, but she just brushed it off. "You're not my father," she said, like the bratty kid actor from a long gone TV show. He'd always assumed the characters on TV exaggerated the traits of real people; his experience with teenage Emiko suggested otherwise. How would his father have dealt with her? Not that the answer to that question would help. As a mere older brother, he could never match the authority of their father.

Nathan heard the front door open and looked toward the bedroom entrance. A moment later Cynthia appeared in the door frame, with a bundle of medicine jars in her hands. She wore a modest sky blue dress — thin at the waist, unrevealing otherwise. Her chestnut brown hair was pulled back and tied in a ponytail. Nathan guessed she was about thirty-five.

"How's our mystery man holding up?" she said, walking over to the bed.

"No change," Nathan said. "Still sleeping like a baby."

Cynthia leaned over and felt the man's forehead.

"No temperature to speak of," she noted.

"Any idea what's wrong with him?" he asked.

"Not the slightest," she replied. "Not yet, anyway."

Nathan watched as Cynthia pulled the sheet down, revealing the man's upper body and his dark plaid shirt that was unraveling at the seams. She felt the man's wrist, checking his vitals. *Cynthia really knows her stuff*, Nathan thought. Technically she was only a nurse, but Frontier View considered her the village doctor. She could dress wounds, set bones, relieve flu symptoms — all the important things.

No, she couldn't work miracles; not that anyone could anymore. Even the best doctors in Duluth had trouble with advanced ailments — a fact Nathan had painstakingly learned. If he could go back in time, to his father's final days, he would have let his dad spend that time at home with friends and family, rather than within the whitewashed confines of the Duluth General Hospital ...

"Earth to Nathan!" Cynthia said, snapping her fingers to get his attention.

"Yeah?" Nathan said as he came out of his daydream, yanking his head back upward.

"I can take it from here," she said with a smile. "And I bet you still have to give Emiko a piece of your mind."

"Don't remind me," Nathan groaned. Why couldn't his sister just grow up? He stood up and headed for the door.

"Thanks for your help, Nathan," Cynthia said.

"Anytime," he replied, nodding at her as he left the room and made his way out of the cabin.

Was it already late afternoon? The sun had sunk low into the western sky, yet the stifling midsummer heat remained. Nathan looked across the way at the row of cabins. Sometimes it still amazed him that he had gone from growing up in Minneapolis to living a quaint hamlet in the middle of the woods. He had long since realized that life in Frontier View wasn't better or worse than the hustle and bustle of Minneapolis — just different, though he did occasionally miss the conveniences of the city. He didn't imagine Frontier View would be implementing a light rail system anytime soon.

He trudged to his cabin, where a confrontation with Emiko awaited. The initial rush of anger had subsided, but it was still his responsibility to try to talk a bit of sense into her. Every time Emiko disappeared, it felt like *The Boy Who Cried Wolf*. Nathan never knew if she had stumbled into trouble or she was just rebelliously gallivanting around the woods.

The cabin door creaked open. On Nathan's left was the entrance to the bedroom. Behind it in the far corner was a kitchen area. The kitchen extended into the dining and living areas that comprised the right half of the homely cabin. Old family photos and a few pieces of childhood artwork adorned the walls, reminders of the days when Nathan was still an elementary school student in the city.

Emiko sat in the same rocking chair where he'd kept his vigil. She was reading a book from the bookshelf behind it, trying to pretend nothing had happened.

"Hey, sis," Nathan greeted.

"Hey, how is Beard?" Emiko replied without looking up from her book.

"*Beard?*" Nathan asked. "That's what you call him?" His sister was *definitely* trying to avoid a serious discussion, but he didn't feel like pushing the issue.

"Well, we don't know his name," she said, setting the book on her lap, "so I figured I'd give him a nickname."

Nathan rolled his eyes. Though the name was oddly endearing ...

"You know, 'Beard' might blow your head off if he hears you call him that." He stepped closer to the rocking chair and looked down at Emiko sternly. "It'd save me the trouble."

Emiko stood up and walked past Nathan.

"What would Mom and Dad think if they saw us now?" she asked, looking at a drawing above the bookcase — a family portrait drawn in crayon, drawn by Emiko many years ago.

"They'd be proud, I'm sure. Happy to see we're getting by," Nathan answered. "What do *you* think?"

"Huh? Since when do you care what *I* think?" Emiko replied.

"Since ... well, since always," Nathan said. "We're in this together, right?"

His sister paused to think.

"I think they'd be proud of us, too," she said.

"Proud of *me,* at least," he said with a grin. "I don't know about *you.* I mean, look at that drawing — you couldn't even spell my name correctly." Wasn't he supposed to be scolding her? And yet here he was, smiling and joking around. At this rate, he'd never rein in her irresponsible teenage escapades.

"That's no fair!" Emiko said, glaring at her brother. "By the way, what's for dinner?"

*Does she really think I don't know what she's doing?* Nathan wondered. He'd let her get away with changing the subject — for now.

"How about squirrel and potato stew?" he suggested.

Emiko grimaced, then gave a reluctant nod.

"Don't look at me like that. I'm just the cook — *you're* the great huntress of Frontier View." Nathan chuckled.

"I *hate* it when you call me that!" Emiko snarled.

"Then shoot some bigger game," Nathan said. Admittedly, eating small game at every meal was growing tiresome.

"Maybe I would, if you'd give me a rifle more powerful than a .22," Emiko suggested.

Nathan shrugged. "Dad would tell you not to make excuses," he said, smirking as he wandered toward the kitchen.

# Chapter 4

"THIS IS THE GENERAL."

"Private Brushnell reporting, sir."

"The trail still warm?"

"More than warm — the situation is heating up, sir."

There was a moment of silence.

"Well, out with it son."

"Er, right — Osborne collapsed in the road this morning. As I approached, a young girl wandered out from the woods and discovered him. After the girl left, a group came to the location and carried Osborne to a nearby village."

"And why didn't you report this to me immediately?"

"I felt it could wait, sir."

"Fair enough. Level-headedness in the field — a good trait to have. What's the name of the village?"

"Frontier View, sir."

"We have an outpost just north of there, on Sawbill Lake."

"Correct, sir."

The general paused before continuing.

"Private, I need your opinion. Tell me, does Osborne appear to have a destination?"

"No, sir. As near as I can tell he's wandering aimlessly, in no hurry to arrive anywhere."

"Alright. In that case, go join the men at Sawbill Lake for the time being."

"What about Osborne?"

"He'll be held up for a bit, I suspect. Just keep tabs on him from afar. I'll give you further instructions tomorrow."

"Understood, sir."

"The General, over and out."

The private gazed at the floor of his pup tent, troubled. This mission was bringing him a bit too close to home. Well, former home. A year ago he'd left Frontier View, vowing never to return. He had no intention of breaking that promise now.

He crawled into this sleeping bag and closed his eyes, content to put off the problem until it came to a head.

# Chapter 5

THE MORNING DEW still glistened on the leaves as Emiko scampered through the forest. Stray droplets of water collected on her long black hair, giving it a moist sheen. She'd set out early, while Nathan was still catching up on his sleep, in order to avoid her brother's dire warnings about the dangers of the forest. What did he know anyway? She spent far more time dashing through the brush and trees than he ever had. Through her childhood and during her father's illness, the woods had remained her only steadfast companion. With the Ruger 10/22 strapped to her back, she had nothing to fear.

Every morning she made rounds, checking her traps to see if they had snared any critters overnight. She leapt over a small log, then fell to her knees to check a box trap, tucked discreetly underneath a raspberry bush.

She swept away the lush green leaves of the bush and looked in the trap. There was nothing inside, not even the bait she'd carefully placed yesterday. She frowned, picking it up to take a closer look.

Her father had bought this trap in Duluth. It was a steel cage with a spring-loaded door that slammed shut when a creature put weight on the center plate that held the bait. Emiko reached her hand inside and wiggled the plate. With a little effort, the door swung shut on her arm. She pried it open and took a closer look. The spring mechanism needed a fresh rub of grease; unfortunately, she didn't have any right now. She put a few breadcrumbs on the plate, seeing as there was still a chance the trap would snap shut on a rodent, then made a mental note to get a little oil from the Frontier View Co-op later.

Sometimes she wondered if Nathan appreciated all the work she did. After all, he only saw the spoils; he didn't see the effort that went into bringing home meat. Checking the traps, sniping small game, making sure her rifle was always in tip-top shape — those were all *her* responsibilities. Yet if she lapsed in even one of those things, she *and* Nathan would have to resort to begging neighbors for food.

Oh sure, Nathan toiled too — mostly in the fields around Frontier View, tending to tubers, collard greens, cabbage ... pretty much whatever would grow. And he took care of gathering firewood, as well as most of the household chores. His role was as important as hers, if not more so. She accepted that. What irked her was that Nathan often said they were "partners" ... but did he treat her like a partner? Emiko surely didn't think so. He still treated her like a kid. Their dad could get away with that, but Nathan? No way.

Stepping lightly, she approached a fallen white pine. It was a massive length of timber with gnarled roots at the base. It had been down for nearly three years now. Before it fell, it would have lorded above the other trees. Now, however, it served as one of her favorite hunting blinds. The elements had gradually eaten away its branches, allowing her to easily rest against it. The location was perfect as well. A bubbling brook weaved through the trees, about a hundred feet north of the log. She could hide behind its wide trunk and watch as game approached to drink at the narrow stream. Occasionally she would sit there all day, observing the wildlife. As a steward of the forest, she prided herself on taking only what she needed.

Emiko yawned. How long had it been since she'd had a decent night's sleep? A little nap couldn't hurt. She took the gun off her back and set it on the decomposing bark of the massive log. Then she leaned against the log and closed her eyes, allowing sleep to take her and thankful that Nathan couldn't pester her here.

* * *

"Disappearing chickens?" Nathan asked, surprised.

"That's right," Pierre answered. "I go out in the morning expecting a couple fresh eggs, only to find that half my chickens are gone!"

*Just my luck*, Nathan thought. He'd come to Pierre's place hoping to get an egg or two in exchange for a scoop of lard.

"I haven't the slightest idea where they're disappearing to. Could be wolves, I suppose? Maybe I'll organize a night watch." Pierre shook his head and let out a sigh. "In any case, I still have a few eggs lying around and the stove's already hot, so how about we share some breakfast?"

"That'd be great." Nathan nodded approvingly. Pierre, a former history professor, was always willing to lend a hand. He was the oldest man in town, with white hair and jowls that resembled a German Boxer's. He stood about as tall as Nathan and sported a slight paunch, yet he was quite spry for his age. Nathan imagined if Frontier View needed a mayor, Pierre would be on the short list.

Pierre took a moment to wipe the thick lenses of his horn-rimmed glasses on his shirt, then began to work on breakfast.

"Let's see ... we have lard and eggs," he said, thinking out loud. "I believe I have an onion or two around here as well ..." he trailed off, as he sifted through a cabinet near his stove.

Pierre's house was even smaller than Nathan's — a single-room cabin. A narrow bed sat to the left of the entrance. On the other side of the door there was a rocking chair, resting near towering stacks of unshelved books, precariously balanced against the wall. The other side of the cabin consisted of cooking and dining space, complete with a wood stove, which also kept the cabin warm in the winter.

"Aha, an onion!" Pierre exclaimed. He brought it to the counter and began to dice it. "So, any updates on our bearded friend?"

"I haven't heard anything from Cynthia," Nathan said, as he put a pan on the stovetop and added a spoonful of lard.

"It must have been quite a shock for Emiko, stumbling across a mysterious stranger like that," said Pierre.

"No, she took it in stride," Nathan said. "Actually, I think she saw it as a chance to escape a scolding. She found him after staying out all night in the woods."

"Is that right?" Pierre said. "Sounds like she's growing up." He walked over to Nathan and tossed the diced onion into the melted lard, now sizzling in the pan that Nathan was tending to.

"If she's growing up, why is she getting harder to deal with?" Nathan asked.

Pierre shrugged his shoulders. "You'd know better than me — I haven't been her age in over 60 years!" he said as he cracked the eggs and let their contents fall into a small porcelain bowl.

Nathan thought back through the last few years. He couldn't recall ever going through a rebellious phase like the one his sister was in now. Between chores and keeping food on the table, he had never had time to disobey his father.

"It's because I'm not doing a good job of looking out for her, isn't it?" Nathan asked, frowning as he watched the onions slowly soften and turn brown.

"Hey now," Pierre said, setting down the eggs he was whisking. "That couldn't be further from the truth. Look, I'm sure Emiko would have given your father just as much trouble as she's giving you."

"You think so?" Nathan wondered aloud.

"Think so? I *know* so. Let me tell you, when your father complained about one of his children, nine times out of ten it was Emiko. And boy, did she give him fits."

"Really?" Nathan looked at Pierre doubtfully. He couldn't picture his father complaining about either of them. In his mind's eye, their father was always unwaveringly firm — equal parts caring and stern.

"Sure. He was amazed at how different you two are," Pierre said. "There was Nathan, the obedient son, and Emiko, the wild child. Er, don't tell her I said that."

Nathan smiled. "Don't worry — your secret's safe with me," he said. "But that doesn't help me. I need to know how my dad would've handled Emiko."

"He'd probably do the same thing you're doing. Do you think he could have stopped Emiko from staying out in the woods through the night?"

Nathan thought for a moment, then shook his head.

"No, I guess not. He'd probably stay up all night and scold her when she finally got home." *Just like I do,* Nathan thought.

"Well, there you have it." Pierre smiled as he poured the whisked eggs over the onion. The raw eggs hissed as they spread across the hot pan. "Unfortunately, that burden falls on you now. Remember though, you're not alone. I can help — as can the other members of our fine community."

"Thanks, Pierre." Nathan nodded weakly. Talking with Pierre was reassuring, yet he still felt uncomfortable. *Maybe I just need to let Emiko have a bit more space*, he thought. However, as much as his sister would like to think otherwise, the woods *were* dangerous, and Nathan wasn't confident that he was doing enough to keep her out of harm's way.

\* \* \*

Emiko heard something rustle nearby and awoke with a start. Her heart throbbed — each beat pulsating through her ears. Instinctively, she felt behind her head. Her rifle was still there, undisturbed. She swung it around her body and rested it in her lap. The rustling had stopped ... *probably just a rodent or a bird hopping through the underbrush.*

How long had she been asleep? Judging from the sun, it was still well before noon. She turned and peeked out above the log. The brook was still there, of course, but a fully matured bull moose, complete with a wide rack of curving antlers, now stood beside it. Spotting a moose wasn't unusual — the burly creatures roamed freely through the woodlands near Frontier View. In fact, sometimes they even passed right through town early in the morning.

Unfortunately, despite Nathan's squawking about how she should bring home more meat, she couldn't justify shooting at the big animal. The bulky carcass would give her trouble — a moose could outweigh her by over 1,000 pounds. More importantly, a .22 rifle wasn't suited for big game hunting — it lacked stopping power. Now, if Nathan would give her a real gun ...

A small object, hanging from a birch tree near the moose caught her eye — a wasp nest. Emiko smirked. If the forest was going to tease her with big game, she'd have to taunt right back. She lifted her gun, resting the barrel on the log. Taking her time, Emiko leveled her sights on the nest, aiming at the top where it connected to the tree.

The moose bent its neck downward to enjoy a drink of fresh stream water. Emiko felt a twinge of guilt at disturbing it, but not enough to stand down. She pulled the trigger and the bullet rang out. The wasp nest broke from the tree and it fell straight down, hitting the ground by the moose's feet.

Unnerved by the gunfire, the moose pulled its mouth from the water, looking out to see where the sound had come from. Then it noticed the angry wasps swarming at its feet. Immediately, it took off, away from the stream and back into the thick of the trees. Emiko snickered, watching as the swarm of wasps grew and chased after the moose. She was lucky the little insects didn't know who'd really knocked down their nest and she intended to keep it that way. Once again, she ducked behind the cover of the log.

After taking a moment to enjoy her small victory over the moose, she poked her head above the log again.

The moose was long gone. In its place was a man. The gunfire must have attracted his attention. He was fair-skinned, short, and portly with a closely shaved head, and he wore a moss green vest over a dark shirt and jeans. His potbelly and stout figure reminded her of the dwarf on the cover of one of Nathan's fantasy novels — though he lacked the beard, of course.

He also had a pistol at his hip, which concerned her — hunters used rifles, not pistols, as the longer barrel of a rifle offered increased accuracy at range. Emiko ducked behind the cover of her log. Had he seen her? It occurred to her that maybe he was looking for Beard.

"Hey, Jeremiah, you reckon where that shot came from?" the man said.

"Nope," another voice responded.

Emiko gulped — the man wasn't alone. Curiosity got the best of her and she took another glimpse over the log. The other man was wading through the shallow stream. He had dark skin and a slender build, also clad in a vest, shirt, and jeans. He cradled a shotgun in his arms.

"Why we comin' this far south, anyway?" asked the dark-skinned man — Jeremiah.

"'Cause we ain't got nothing else to do," replied the heftier man. "Who knows? Maybe we can snatch a few more chickens tonight."

"If you say so," Jeremiah said with a shrug. "Where'd Dwayne go?"

"Hell if I know," said the portly man.

*Yes, where did Dwayne go?* Emiko wondered. She had three armed men closing in on her position. And ... her rifle! Swiftly, she reached one arm above the log and pulled it back toward her. It thudded softly against the log.

"Barry, you hear that?" Jeremiah asked.

His partner — Barry — smirked.

"I sure did," he said. Then his mischievous eyes fell on Emiko.

*Moose pie!* Emiko dove behind the cover of the log.

"Hey little girlie, we won't hurt you," Barry called out to her.

*They think I'm a dumb little girl? I'll show them!* she thought. What were her options? She wasn't going to just give herself up — the men looked about as trustworthy as a pair of hungry wolves. That left her with two choices: run or fight. *No reason to hide,* she thought — they knew where she was. She stood up from behind the log.

"Hey there darling, what's your name?" Barry asked, as he stepped through the brush, inching closer.

"Who's asking?"

"A friend."

"A friend?"

"That's right, honey," Barry said. "Your dad sent us to out to look for you. He's really worried."

Emiko just glared at him.

"Aw, what's that look for?" he said, trying to sound hurt. He and Jeremiah continued to approach, now about twenty feet away.

"Sorry, my dad's dead," Emiko said. "And I don't think he was friends with any losers like you."

Barry growled.

"Hear that, Jeremiah?" he said. "This one's a real live wire."

"I heard it alright," Jeremiah said.

The men were close and inching closer. If Emiko didn't act soon, she'd be at their mercy.

"One more step and you're dead," she said, shouldering her rifle and aiming at Barry. Would they buy her bluff? She choked down her unease. She'd seen thousands of dead and dying in her lifetime, but she'd never had reason to point her gun at a human before.

"Hey now, we don't want any trouble," Barry said, raising his hands in the air.

"Then you'll turn around and walk away," she said.

"Okay, darling, easy now," Barry said. He and Jeremiah slowly turned around, then gingerly began to creep off in the opposite direction.

Emiko grinned — she was in control now.

"And don't forget to say 'Hi' to the other dwarves for me," she said.

"Why you little," Barry growled, as he spun around and started toward her. "A twerp like you ain't gonna shoot me."

*Bear scat!* Emiko's heart throbbed. She gripped her Ruger tightly as Barry continued toward her. He was still holding his gun up in the air. She didn't know what he'd do to her and she wasn't eager to find out.

She closed her eyes and pulled the trigger. The shot rang out like a firecracker.

"Cocksucker!" Barry wailed.

Emiko opened her eyes. Barry was writhing on the ground in pain, holding his leg. Jeremiah had turned around and was aiming his gun at her. Panicking, she ducked behind the cover of the log. She had to figure out how to disable Jeremiah, quickly! She'd shot one man. Surely she could shoot another ...

Then she heard a twig snap behind her. As she turned to look, something heavy slammed into her skull and she fell to the ground, unconscious.

# Chapter 6

"THIS IS THE GENERAL."

"Private Brushnell reporting, sir."

"Calling in early today, I see."

"I have a situation here, sir."

"I'm all ears."

"Our other three men, stationed here at Sawbill Lake — today they brought in a young girl. There's talk of holding her hostage for a small ransom."

"You didn't feel the need to report to me immediately when Osborne collapsed — why now, soldier?"

*He has a point*, the private admitted to himself. He was anxious because he knew the victim, but he shouldn't have let that affect his judgment.

"I'm sorry, sir."

"No need to apologize, son. I'm glad you called in — we can use this situation to our advantage."

"We can, sir?"

"Yes. You see, as much as Osborne appears to enjoy aimless drifting, I know what he loves even more."

"What's that, sir?"

"The impossible."

The private paused for a moment.

"What are you suggesting, sir?"

"Keep the girl hostage, but don't ask for an easily payable ransom — request an exorbitant, impossible sum. It will get

Osborne's attention and he'll come up your way — I guarantee it."

"And then?"

"I have some information for you to communicate to him. I need you to pass it on, while keeping my name out of it. I'll get it to you as soon as I can confirm a few details."

"Understood, sir. What action should we take until then?"

"Just sit tight. Osborne is as tough as they come — he'll be on his feet again soon. Prepare an anonymous ransom note and deliver it in a day or two. I trust you to take care of the details, Private. My records say you're from that area. Use that knowledge to your advantage."

"Yes, sir."

"The General, over and out."

With a sigh, the private relaxed his grip on the handheld radio, letting it hit the table. When he'd discovered that Barry, Jeremiah, and Dwayne had been plundering minor things from Frontier View, he didn't raise a fuss, but this was different. Not that he had ever been particularly close to Emiko ... something just felt wrong. Weren't they supposed to be dispensing law and order across the land?

*I should trust the General,* he thought. If this is what it took to bring civilization back to the world, then he'd accept it as a necessary evil. In the meantime, a part of him hoped Barry would succumb to a bacterial infection. The General's army had no need for redneck scum.

# Chapter 7

*I'M ALL ALONE NOW,* Nathan thought.

Emiko had been gone for nearly three full days. She'd disappeared before he woke up, three mornings ago. When she didn't return that night, he'd felt angry. When she didn't come home the next night, he'd grown worried. Then, this morning, he'd set out alone, heading into the woods to look for her. Afternoon and evening passed without him finding a trace of his sister, and now he was still foolishly searching deep into the night.

The moon was almost full, but the dense foliage above captured most of its light, leaving hardly any for Nathan. His eyelids felt like bags of sand, hanging over his eyes as he struggled to remain vigilant.

"Emiko!" he cried out. His voice echoed through the forest, fading as it reverberated around him. An owl, perched somewhere in the darkness above, hooted in reply before silently flying into the night. Nathan stopped and listened carefully to the forest. The only sound he heard was his own heartbeat, pounding in his ears. It felt like he was passing through a jungle on the dark side of the moon — a silent wonderland.

"Emiko!" he yelled again, his voice growing more desperate. This time, not even the owl answered. Dead silence.

A cool wind began whistling between the branches of the trees. This far north, even the late summer nights could be brisk. Nathan crossed his arms, pulling them in toward his chest for warmth as he continued his search.

Shortly he came to a clearing in the tree cover. He took advantage of the opportunity to examine the cloudless night sky, picking out the constellations among the twinkling stars. Each one had a story to go with it, and Nathan recollected the stories his father had shared as they gazed at the stars together. From the labors of Hercules to the travails of Perseus and Andromeda, the myths and legends flowed through his mind. Individually, each star was just a tiny point in the sky, but working together, they composed the original storybook — a record of history, dating back to the dawn of time.

*Maybe Emiko is looking up at the stars, too*, he thought. If only she could give him a sign ... a signal that she was near.

A shooting star whizzed across the skyline, leaving a long, hazy trail in its wake before fading completely. Nathan shook his head. The stars were beautiful, but they couldn't help him. He raised his hands to his mouth.

"Emiko!" he called out. *It's no use,* he thought. His sister wasn't out here, and even if she were, he wouldn't find her searching alone by moonlight.

*What did I do to deserve this?* he wondered, sighing deeply, as he fell to his knees in exhaustion. He closed his eyes and knelt in silence, drifting in the space between sleep and meditation. His mind went blank and time slipped away.

*Emiko, where are you?* he silently pleaded. *I can't do this without you.* If only he had respected her more — known how to deal with her, like his father would have ...

Nathan slowly opened his eyes. The sky was brightening and the stars had already begun to fade. Had he really searched all through the night? Gathering his strength, he found the will to pick himself up off the ground and began the trek home, carefully avoiding the branches and rocks underfoot as they scraped at his heavy boots.

Frontier View would send out a search party soon, but he knew it would be in vain. He was alone now. The Desolation had claimed his mom, his dad had succumbed to cancer, and now he'd lost his sister. Who would leave next? *Best not to think about it,* he thought. Mindlessly, he continued putting one foot in front of the other. Frontier View was just around the bend.

A few minutes later, he could see the cabins. Keeping his head low, he trudged toward home. The crest of the sun was just visible above the trees as he reached his door.

As Nathan entered, he eyed a folded sheet of paper, unexpectedly lying in the middle of the cabin's main room among the other clutter. *It looks like a herd of cattle stampeded through here,* he thought, making a hazy mental note to tidy up in the morning. After veering left into the bedroom, he collapsed forward onto his bed, still clothed. His head hit the pillow and his body refused to move another inch.

What now? He didn't know what he could do anymore ...

"I can't do this alone," he mumbled to no one in particular, before falling into a long, dreamless sleep.

# Chapter 8

"HOLD YOUR HORSES! Don't you at least want your clothes back?"

John stormed out the door, ignoring Cynthia as she called after him. A light breeze passed through his loose fitting gown and tickled his underside.

The last time he'd woken up in an unfamiliar bed, he'd found himself alone in an abandoned underground military hospital. He'd surfaced, only to discover a godforsaken version of the world he'd remembered. *This*, however, was something entirely different. He reached for his gun, but his hand found only white linen. Of course — they would have removed his gun belt when they took off the rest of his clothes.

"What the hell is this place?" he asked, turning back to Cynthia. "A set for *Little Town in the Big Woods*?"

"How about you come back inside and get yourself decent — I'll explain everything," she said.

*Well, she does have my gun and my pack*, John realized. That left him no choice.

"Fine," he said, begrudgingly allowing Cynthia to usher him back inside.

\* \* \*

"This is the best soup I've had in ages," John said. He couldn't recall the last time he'd tasted anything so thick and velvety. As he ate, his memories gradually came back to him, from the voracious hunger to his encounter with the frankenmoose.

After he finished the bowl of soup, he set it down on the table and turned back to his hostess.

"So, who found me?" he asked.

"A neighbor of mine — a girl named Emiko," Cynthia said.

"Emiko?"

"It's Japanese. Her father was second generation Japanese-American, I think," Cynthia said as she sat back in her chair. "Emiko told us about you, and so we sent a little rescue party to help."

As he listened to Cynthia explain everything, John finally began to feel at ease. Fortunately, he hadn't woken up in a hospital — he hated everything about them, from the stark white walls to the pervasive smell of death that lingered in every nook and cranny. The cozy cabin made him feel much more at home. As for the village outside ... well, it wasn't the first one of its kind that he'd seen, but it was certainly the most rustic. *Every* home built in log cabin style? Even considering the state of the world, the village was an anachronism.

"Get many visitors up here?" he asked.

"Occasionally we get traders in from Duluth, but no, other than that not many people make it up this way," Cynthia said. "This area used to be a government protected wilderness — as far as I know, there isn't another village north of here until you get into Canada."

"Wish I had known that *before* I crossed the border," he said.

"You know, there's this thing called a *map*," she said with a tiny smirk. "What led you down here, anyway?"

John shrugged.

"A drifter, huh? Where from?" she asked.

It seemed the farther west he came, the more ridiculous people found his answer to be. Still, he had no reason to hide the truth.

"I'm from Maine," he said.

"Maine?" she asked. She sounded only slightly surprised. "That's a pretty long hike, isn't it?"

"You bet," he said with a nod. It had taken him nearly two years to get this far, though for someone walking directly and purposefully, it wouldn't have taken more than a few months.

"By the way, I have a personal question, if you don't mind ..." Cynthia trailed off, waiting for his assent.

"Go ahead," he said, reluctantly. He didn't much like talking about himself.

"How did you get the scar around your left shoulder?" she asked.

John scowled — he'd forgotten that Cynthia had changed his clothes and undoubtedly had seen his replacement arm. Outwardly, it could have passed for the original, if it weren't for the thick ring of pink scar tissue that circled around his shoulder.

"You don't wanna know," he muttered.

"A real man of mystery," Cynthia replied with an easy smile. "So, what's your plan now?"

"Keep walking, I suppose," he said.

"Where to?" she asked.

"South, I guess," he said with a shrug.

"Well, don't rush yourself out the door — stick around for a while, until you're at one hundred percent. I'm still not sure why you fainted," she said.

John mulled the offer over. She had a point — why he had collapsed was unclear, and he wasn't on a deadline to arrive at any particular place. Maybe it would be best if he stayed put for a bit ...

"I'll consider it," John replied. "In the meantime, I'm gonna get some fresh air," he said, pointing to the door with a grin. "Now that I'm fully clothed and all." Just to be sure, he felt at his holster — the Colt was there. He picked it up in his hand and swung open the cylinder. It was loaded with six shells. He pointed the muzzle toward the ceiling, letting one shell slide into his lap as he held the other five in, shutting the cylinder afterward. He pocketed the sixth bullet.

"Who gave me the ammo?" he asked.

"Oh, just a gift from the people here," Cynthia answered. "We have plenty in storage. Just ask if you need more."

"Thanks. I appreciate it," John said, as he stood up and headed for the door.

* * *

Once again, John stepped outside, this time examining the little hamlet more closely. It looked like men with axes had come through and cut a giant, rectangular swath out of the forest, creating space for the cabins. The entrance to Cynthia's home faced southward; from what he could tell, all of the cabins faced each other in two rows running east-west. On either end of the rows he could see where the forest began again, separating civilization and the wild. The long, wide area between the homes served as a main street, covered in a mixture of grass, weeds, and dirt. It was much like he imagined a town from the Old West would look, with lush green trees and heavily insulated log cabins substituting for the arid desert and thinly constructed buildings.

John could see a few children, shouting and kicking up dust with their heels as they played a game — baseball, perhaps? One kid was throwing a small ball; another swung at it with a crude bat. John looked on as the pitcher, a boy about ten, wound up and hurled the ball toward the hitter. The hitter's stick connected with the ball, driving it into the air. John lost track of it in the sun's glare, then heard it hit the ground somewhere behind him. He turned around to find it.

"Home run!" the hitter called out. John spotted the ball, obscured by the grass, and trotted over to pick it up. It was a crude approximation of a baseball, round and wrapped with leather.

By the time John turned around to toss it back to the group, the pitcher had already caught up to him. The pitcher looked at John's unfamiliar face with curiosity.

"Did you kids make this baseball on your own?" John asked, as he gave the ball a light toss to get a feel for it.

"My dad made it. Cut a wood core and then wrapped some deerskin around it. Works just like the old ones, he says," the boy replied.

*I'm not sure about that, but it is surprisingly well made,* John mused to himself.

"You're the man they found a couple days ago, aren't you?" the boy asked, squinting warily at the bearded man.

"That's right, son," John replied.

"You aren't from around here, are you?" the boy said.

"No, I'm not," John said as he gave the ball another toss. "I'm from out east. Just passing through."

"East? You mean like, Grand Marais?" the boy asked.

"Nope, try again," John replied. "Farther east."

The boy looked slightly puzzled, then his eyes filled with awe. "You're from Thunder Bay?"

John chuckled. *The world sure has become a whole lot smaller.*

"Nope, farther east yet. Have you heard of Maine?" he said.

The boy shook his head.

"Well, if you start here and keep heading east," John directed, pointing opposite the western sun, "you'll get there eventually. Can't say I'd recommend walking there though — there's a lot of rough country between here and the eastern seaboard." He turned back to the boy. "Ask your parents about it when you get a chance. They'll know something about Maine."

"Sure thing, mister," the boy said, his eyes drifting down toward John's hand. "Can I have my ball back now?"

"Sure," he said, handing the ball over, "here you go." The kid thanked him and ran back to rejoin the other children. As John meandered past the group, he couldn't help but smile at their conversation.

"It's somewhere in Canada, I tell ya!"

"No way, I bet it's just past Grand Marais!"

"Don't you guys know your history? Maine was one of the fifty states, before the Desolation."

*History?* Referring to Maine in the past tense still felt unnatural to John. If he closed his eyes, he could still smell the salty Atlantic air and hear the mewing gulls along the shoreline. He imagined the smooth, creamy texture of clam chowder tickling his tongue. Not even Cynthia's pork bone soup could match a hearty bowl of chowder.

Maine was still where it had always been. Only the cities and villages stood empty now. John's friends and family? All gone, as far as he knew. He saw no reason to return to the coast. The wilderness was his home now.

Continuing through the village, he noticed that two larger buildings end-capped both rows of cabins. Curious about their purpose, he walked toward the one on the southern row, opposite Cynthia's side.

Despite being only one story, the building felt massive compared to the cabins John had just passed. A sign above the door read "Frontier View Co-op," printed in thick, green uppercase letters. To the side of the door sat a small bench. A sharp V-shaped roof rested on top of the building, constructed from assorted pieces of sheet metal. It was haphazardly screwed and nailed onto the wooden frame, giving it the appearance of a patchwork quilt.

A fence sat to the building's right side. The overpowering smell of animal dung suggested it was a stable. John walked over to take a peek. Then he saw *it* — the frankenmoose! No, three of the buggers! They turned to look at him. He stumbled backward in surprise, swallowing a gasp. His arms crawled with goose bumps.

"What the hell are those things!" he exclaimed.

"Never seen a tvapa before?" a man's voice responded. John's body jerked in surprise, turning to meet the voice. A white haired man with glasses was standing beside him. The man wore a long-sleeved green shirt and khakis. John took him to be about seventy.

"Oh, I've seen one alright," John said. "Had myself a little sparring match with him."

The man raised an eyebrow at John, quizzically.

"Sparring match?" he said.

"You heard me. These franken ..." John hesitated. "Frankenmeese? I just don't trust 'em. Something about their eyes."

The old man blinked, then paused for a moment, as if searching for the correct response. Then he shrugged and offered his hand.

"I'm Pierre."

"John. John Osborne." The two shook and then released hands.

"Cynthia cleared you to get out of bed?" Pierre said, leaning closer to carefully examine John's eyes.

John scowled in reply.

"Hey, just making sure!" Pierre said, raising his hands defensively as he took a step back. "Sorry, I've just never known tvapas to be violent creatures."

"Well," John said, "it didn't exactly attack me, but ..."

Pierre chuckled. "No worries — I'll take your word for it," he said. "So, how are you feeling?"

"Better, I think," John said, stroking his beard. *Not that I have the slightest idea why I collapsed in the first place.*

"I like the beard, by the way," Pierre offered. "Definitely not a style that's encouraged these days, but to me a beard evokes the great American heroes of yore. You know, Lincoln, Grant, Lee ..." He paused, shaking his head. "I bet most kids these days don't even know who Lincoln is — truly a shame."

*Lincoln, huh?* he thought. He'd never heard a compliment about his beard — not a one — until now. He stood in silence, mulling it over.

"There's a tavern, Loon's Landing, up this way," Pierre said, pointing behind the Co-op. "How about we grab a drink? I'd love to hear what's going on elsewhere in the world."

"Sure," John said with a shrug. "I could use a hearty glass of whiskey."

# Chapter 9

NATHAN RUBBED HIS tired, swollen eyes as he sat up in bed. Bright rays of midday sunlight streamed in through the window. Glancing over at the other bed, Nathan remembered that Emiko was gone; her bedspread remained tidy and undisturbed, just as he'd made it for her three mornings ago.

With a groan, he swung his feet off the bed. Searching through the night had left his body exhausted. He sighed, realizing he hadn't taken off his boots; their muddy soles had stained the bedspread. *Just another mess to clean*, Nathan thought. How had the cabin become *messier* without Emiko around? After all, *he* always cleaned up after *her*, not the other way around.

His stomach growled, like a bear coming out of hibernation. When was the last time he'd eaten? Not since yesterday morning, at least. He wandered out of the bedroom, past the front door and the rocking chair, and into the kitchen. Looking through the cupboards, he found only a few potatoes — he'd have to get more food soon.

As he walked over to the cast-iron stove to start a fire for cooking, a sheet of paper lying on the floor caught his attention. Ah, right — he'd spotted it last night ... no, this morning, when he'd come home.

The paper was folded in half. Nathan picked it up and looked it over. It was a wide-ruled page from a spiral notebook. No factories mass produced notebooks anymore, yet they were easy enough to find, cluttering shelves and desks unused. He turned the paper over and unfolded it, revealing a handwritten note. His eyes grew wide as he read the words, clenching the paper with his fingernails. *What!?* After taking a deep breath and relaxing his hands, he carefully went through the message again.

*To Whom It May Concern,*

*We have the girl in our custody. If you want her back, bring $5,000 to our outpost on the north end of Sawbill Lake, tomorrow by sundown. We take the money, you take the girl — no problems.*

*P.S. Come alone — keep Osborne out of this.*

Ransom! What the Desolation had Emiko stumbled into? He was relieved to know she was alive, but two new questions plagued him: Where could he get $5,000, and who was "Osborne?"

He crammed the note into his pocket and ran out the door, grabbing his cap on the way out to hide his disheveled hair.

The only activity outside was a group of kids playing ball. A few years ago he would have joined them, but the time for games had passed. He was an adult now and he had to act like one.

A few steps out the door he realized he had no idea where his feet were taking him. *Focus, Nathan,* he thought. *Who can help you with this?* Deciding Pierre would be as good as anyone, Nathan dashed off to find the old professor.

\* \* \*

"So, you don't know anything about this?" Pierre asked, jabbing at the paper with his finger.

53

"Nothing," John replied. Why couldn't he ever enjoy a drink in peace?

Not that Loon's Landing was much of a place. He'd have trouble enjoying a drink there even without Pierre badgering him about the note. Mildew crept up the walls and it was so dark he could barely see his whiskey glass. Presently, the bartender was circumnavigating the room, lighting oil lanterns in each corner. *About damn time*, John thought.

"Let me see the note," he said. "I'd like to know what it is I'm being accused of."

Pierre handed it to him with a reluctant sigh.

The note felt crisp in John's hands. He tilted it until he found the best angle to capture the lamplight. The penmanship was clear, the message brief. And there it was — his name mentioned in the postscript.

"They used my name — so what?" John said, shrugging it off. The appearance of his name *did* concern him, but for now he wouldn't let on. "The more important question is: how are you gonna deal with this?" He turned to the boy — Nathan.

"This is your sister?" he asked.

Nathan nodded. "Emiko is the one who found you in the road," he added, softly.

"Is paying the five grand an option?" John asked.

Nathan shook his head.

"Can Frontier View come up with $5,000?" John asked Pierre. It didn't seem like an outrageous sum.

Pierre shook his head. "Impossible," he said. "Hmm ... you said you came in from Canada, right?"

"From Maine through Canada, yeah," John said.

"Then I suppose you aren't familiar with our currency," Pierre said, as he reached for his wallet and pulled out a blue bill. "The kidnappers aren't asking for greenbacks — their value collapsed along with the U.S. government. We use these now." He handed the banknote to John.

John scanned the features of the strange blue bill. The number five occupied each corner and a proud black bear adorned the center of the front face. He flipped it over, looking at the image that spanned the backside. The rising sun hung in the upper right corner, its light radiating down upon a lone man in a canoe, as he paddled toward the dawn of a new day. John turned to the front again and noted the fine print:

THIS NOTE IS LEGAL TENDER FOR ALL DEBTS, PUBLIC AND PRIVATE

Followed by:

ISSUED BY AUTHORITY OF THE REPUBLIC OF MINNESOTA — DULUTH, MN

The imagery all looked very professional — on par with pre-Desolation paper money, though it seemed to lack any of the advanced security features that twenty-first century U.S. currency had been known for.

As John continued looking over the bill, Pierre began to explain.

"You could knock off a bank in Duluth and you might not find 5,000 MND," he said, assuming a professorial tone. "You see, the people have been slow to readopt fiat currency, a problem owing itself to numerous factors. First, after the rampant inflation that plagued the US dollar — even before the Desolation — the populace is hesitant to put its trust in paper money."

The old man paused for a moment to catch his breath, then continued, "Furthermore, when the population was suddenly reduced one-hundred fold, it greatly diminished the need for 'stores of value.' Now that we no longer have the energy infrastructure to support the opulence of an overbearing aristocracy, the superfluous sums of money that the market formerly distributed unevenly to signify the divide between rich and poor no longer serve any purpose. Thus, the need for currency has contracted exponentially with the reduction in population rather than linearly, and the Republic of Minnesota has acted accordingly, leading to the predicament we now find ourselves in."

John raised an eyebrow at Pierre, silently returning the five-dollar bill. He'd lost the thread of Pierre's mumbo jumbo after the first sentence.

"Excuse me, acute case of the rambles." Pierre rubbed the back of his neck. "You can leave academia, but it will never leave you ..."

"Alright then," John said, picking up the ransom note from the counter, "what's the plan?"

Pierre pursed his lips, offering no reply; Nathan stared at the ground, avoiding eye contact — not exactly the response John had hoped for. He waited for a moment, then offered his plan.

"Here's the deal," John said, looking at Nathan. The boy didn't take his eyes off the floor. "I don't know who delivered this, but I think they're using your sister to get to me — that's not fair. Also," he said, turning to Pierre, "your people gave me a hand when I needed it — I owe you one.

"So," John said, setting the ransom note on the counter, "I'll take care of this. I'll find out who delivered this note and I'll get your sister back." The words invigorated him — it felt like he was taking on a critical mission from HQ, though this time he was acting of his own volition.

"You will?" Pierre sounded relieved.

"Sure thing. I'll get her back faster than you can unload a six-shooter." He patted at the ivory-plated handle of his Colt.

Nathan picked his eyes up off the floor, finally ready to speak.

"I'm coming with you," he said, standing with tense shoulders and his fists clenched at his sides, as though he was mustering all of his will to force out the words.

"I don't think so, son," John said. "I work better alone — no sidekick necessary."

"But she's *my* sister," Nathan said.

"So?" John said, shrugging his shoulders.

Nathan narrowed his eyes.

"I entrusted my dad's life to an 'expert' — I won't make the same mistake twice," he said.

John paused to think it over. He took a long look at Nathan, taking him in from head to toe. The kid was scrawny, like a beanpole with arms sticking out of a grimy white t-shirt. Probably knew how to shoot, but not likely to have any combat experience. His eyes, however, flared with determination, and John wasn't one to underestimate a rookie.

"Fine, you win," John said. "Meet me in front of the Co-op in five minutes and we'll talk shop."

The tension in Nathan's face and shoulders dissipated as he nodded in agreement. Then he walked out of the tavern without another word.

"What's with the kid?" John asked, gesturing toward the door with his head.

"He lost his dad, Ryota, to stomach cancer last year," Pierre said. "Took the poor guy to a doctor, all the way down in Duluth, but it didn't do any good." Pursing his lips, the old man shook his head. "I think he holds himself responsible, even though there was nothing he could've done. He's a sharp kid, but his confidence has taken quite a hit."

John nodded, mulling it over. He grabbed his whiskey and took a sip, grimacing as it trickled down his throat.

"Should I take him with me?" he asked.

Pierre tilted his head slightly to one side and stroked his chin. "I don't want him to get hurt ... but I don't want to see him moping around town, either. Can't say he's much of a fighter, but he does good work when he puts his mind to something," he said.

"Roger that. I'll go talk to him a bit more — make sure he knows what he's signing up for," John said.

"Go ahead," Pierre replied. "I got your drink covered — you didn't exactly get the chance to enjoy it."

John smirked.

"I'm not sure *enjoy* is the word I'd choose," he said, as he stood up and headed for the door.

\* \* \*

Nathan anxiously paced back and forth in front of the Frontier View Co-op. A single oil lamp cast an orange glow on his skin. Though the Co-op was open only from early morning until dusk, the proprietor, Tom, kept a front light on for a couple hours after dark as a courtesy. The cabins in town gradually lit up, one by one. Nathan watched as light flickered through their windows.

He tapped his foot nervously. Where was John? Nathan was having second thoughts about this rescue mission. He didn't know anything about action, combat, or war. What help would he be?

Looking down the row of cabins, he picked out his own unlit home. Its darkened windows made it stand out like a missing tooth in an otherwise perfect smile. *No*, he thought, *I need to be strong. For Emiko's sake as well as for my own.* He suppressed his fidgety foot and stood tall — shoulders back, chest out. No turning back.

Nathan heard quiet footsteps in the distance. He watched as John slowly stepped into the lamplight, which gradually revealed his features. The reflection of the reddish-orange flame glowed in the bearded man's eyes — the only motion on his otherwise expressionless face. Though he stood only an inch or two taller than Nathan, he carried himself like an iron giant, as though nothing could stand between him and his destination.

"Hey son, grab a seat," he offered, pointing to the bench in front of the Co-op.

"Yes, sir," Nathan replied.

John tilted his head slightly to one side.

"I didn't hear you call me 'sir' in that dump of a bar — what changed?" he asked.

"I don't know, sir."

"Well, I don't like it."

"Why not, s —"

"Hammersnap, son! Will you cut that out? If you're going to be any help to me, I need you to be a partner, not a subordinate." He paused to collect himself, then held out his hand. "The name's John Osborne. Call me John."

Nathan fought the urge to grimace as John's iron grip crushed his hand.

"Nathan. Nathan Kanno."

The wooden bench creaked as they sat down.

"So, tell me, son — what's your weapon of choice?" John asked.

"Weapon of choice?" Nathan wondered aloud. "Ah, I use my dad's old Remington 870." The phrase caught him off guard. He thought of the shotgun as a tool, not a weapon.

"Solid gun," John said, as he pantomimed raising a gun to his shoulder. "Pump action, plenty of stopping power — you're a good hand with it?"

Nathan nodded.

"Alright. And you understand the risk involved?" John asked. "There's no shame in having second thoughts."

Nathan paused for a moment — no, he didn't fully know what he was getting into, but did it matter? Nervous as he was, this was something he had to do.

"I understand," he said.

"Good. Then let's talk details. First things first — I'm assuming Sawbill Lake is nearby?" John asked.

"Yeah — about 10 miles north. We go there tomorrow ... then what?" Nathan said.

"Then we find the kidnappers, maybe shoot a few bullets, and get your sister back," John said.

Nathan waited for further explanation. It didn't come.

"*That's* your plan?" he blurted out. "I could have thought of that!"

John shrugged his shoulders. "Do you have a better idea? Unless you have five grand sitting around, my plan is the only plan."

Nathan bit the corner of his lip, then nodded in agreement. The bearded man had a point.

"Next, supplies — you have a gun," John said, lifting his index finger. "Do you have a map of the lake?"

"I have one at home," Nathan said. "Do you want me to go fetch it now?"

"No, it can wait until tomorrow," John said as he held up a second finger. "How about a canoe and paddles?"

"Sure, I have an aluminum canoe sitting behind the cabin," Nathan said. Everyone in Frontier View had a canoe, or at least had access to one. Roads and trails still guided travelers between most towns and villages, but they didn't go everywhere. Canoeing across lakes often proved to be easier than trying to bushwhack a path through the surrounding woodland and Sawbill Lake was no exception.

"Great," John said, raising his ring finger. "Finally, do you have a cart and a ... frankenmoose?"

*Did he shudder as he said that?* Nathan wondered. *No — must've been my imagination. This guy doesn't look like he'd be afraid of anything.*

"A tvapa?" Nathan asked.

"Yeah, one of those," John said. "You have one?"

"No, but given the circumstances, I can probably borrow one from Cynthia. A cart, too." Carrying a canoe to Sawbill Lake was out of the question. Holding a canoe over one's shoulders and walking just one mile was hard work — ten was unthinkable.

"By the way, does their manure always smell so bad?" John asked.

Nathan thought about it a moment. "I guess you get used to it," he said.

John shook his head and let out a deep breath. He raised his pinkie finger, then closed his hand and pumped his fist.

"Sounds like we're set. If you have food that's easy to carry, bring it along, but if not we can do a little hunting along the way. Pack anything else you think we'll need for an overnight trip — try to keep it light," he said.

Nathan rolled his eyes. *Does he think I'm the pampered prince of Frontier View?* "I guess that means I'll have to leave my makeup case and pewter collection behind. Woe is me."

To Nathan's surprise, John grinned at the sarcasm. "You got spunk kid. I like that," he said, pointing his finger at Nathan. Then as if thinking aloud, he added, "Though it's always the spunky ones that want to shoot me."

"You've been shot at before?" Nathan asked.

John merely chuckled in reply.

*Loons over the moon! Who laughs about being shot at?* Nathan wondered.

"Prepare everything on our checklist and meet here at sunup tomorrow. Not a moment later — got it?" John said.

"Got it," Nathan replied with a nod and a tired sigh.

The bench creaked again as John stood up.

"Keep your head up, kid," he said, as he sauntered out of the lamplight, back into the darkness.

# Chapter 10

HOURS LATER, John rested on his unzipped sleeping bag, staring up at the glowing ceiling of his tent, illuminated by the stars and the moon. Not wanting to impose upon Cynthia, he'd set up camp in the woods on the outskirts of Frontier View. Moreover, the thick walls of a cabin dulled the senses and offered a false sense of security — through the thin nylon tent, he could detect any oncoming danger early and act accordingly.

With his right hand, he massaged the lumpy scar tissue around his left shoulder. It still felt strange to his fingertips, like someone had branded him, separating his arm from the rest of his body. Was the arm a gift? A curse? What was its immense power intended for? Whoever gave it to him probably didn't think he'd be using it to sucker punch wild game in the wilderness.

John took a deep breath through his nose — strange, there was something in the air …

*Smoke.*

He poked his head out of the tent. Voices shouted in the distance. With haste, he clothed himself and stepped out to look.

The shadowy trees loomed over him as he passed through the underbrush, towards the village. Thorns clawed at his jeans and low hanging branches slapped at his eyes. As he approached Frontier View, the voices became clearer. "Fire!" he heard. "Pierre's chicken coop is on fire!"

*Well, pull my trigger,* John thought. He steeled himself and picked up his pace, lurching over the roots and downed logs in the darkness, like a blind man dancing through an obstacle course. A jagged piece of bark clipped his shoulder, claiming a shred of his flannel shirt. He leapt over a final bush and fell to one knee, catching his breath as he tried to determine the location of the fire.

The smell of smoke was unmistakable now. An aura of flame danced in the distance. *Out of the woods and into the fire pit,* he thought, standing up and dashing toward the light. Every building he passed was constructed of wood. If the fire got out of hand, it would quickly ravage the entire village.

As he approached, he saw men, women, and children — many half-clothed or in pajamas — scurrying across the village with buckets full of water, like panicked ants defending their hill. Pierre was among them, clearly straining his old body to keep up.

Embers and ashes flitted through the air, carried by drafts of hot air. Through a gap between the houses, John saw the source of the flames — a chicken coop nestled against the rear of Pierre's home. He drew himself closer, watching as a villager braved the sweltering heat and tossed water on the fire. Even standing ten feet back, the blaze seared John's skin.

"What are you standing around for? Grab a bucket and get to work!" a young man shouted over the crackling of the fire. Sweat dripped from his dark mop of hair as he ran up and thrust a bucket at John.

*No, more water won't help — this fire is already burning too hot,* John thought as he stared into the flames. There had to be another way.

The man dropped the bucket at John's feet and barked an admonishment, then spun off.

John quickly surveyed the chicken coop. It was constructed of thin, roughly cut pine, propped up by half-foot stilts and separated from the cabin by an arm's length.

His eyes darted back and forth as he examined the resources at hand. Buckets, trees, dirt and grass, an axe, a chain — it was like an algebra problem with a multitude of variables, to which there may or may not be a workable solution.

Pierre ran by John, drenched with sweat. He tossed a bucket of water on the fire and turned back to get more.

"Pierre!" John shouted.

The old man slowed and looked toward John.

"Oh, it's you!" Pierre said. "Pick up that bucket and help us out!" As he began to take off again, John grasped his shoulder.

"Listen to me," John demanded gruffly.

Pierre looked into John's eyes for a moment, pursing his lips before nodding anxiously.

"Your little buckets aren't gonna put out this fire before it spreads," John said, pointing to the cabin. The flames from the coop licked at the larger building, as though they were whetting their appetite for the main course. "I have a plan — do you trust me?"

Pierre paused for a moment, then gave a reluctant nod. "Okay, but make it quick," he said.

"Round up two tvapas, put a yoke on 'em, and bring them over here," John ordered. "I'll take care of the rest. We don't have much time. Go!"

Still clinging tightly to his bucket, Pierre nodded a final time then took off in an awkward jog.

"What the hell are you doing standing there? Pick up the bucket and get to work!" a voice shrieked.

John looked back. It was the same young man from before. John gave him the evil eye — the meanest scowl his bearded face could muster. The man cursed and threw his hands in the air, again running to fetch more water. *If this doesn't work, I'll be chased out of town by an enraged bucket brigade*, John thought to himself.

Pierre returned sooner than expected, leading two tvapas by a rope in his hands.

"I hope you know what you're doing," he said.

"Always," John said with a smirk. "Just bring 'em over there, in front of the chicken coop."

John ran to the adjacent cabin and reached for a length of steel chain coiled against the outer wall. With both arms, he heaved the heavy chain onto the ground. He grabbed hold of one hooked end and dashed toward the tvapas. The chain links followed behind him, slithering through the grass like a snake after its prey. He attached the chain's hook to the tvapas' yoke. The burly creatures stood about five yards from the burning chicken coop. Neither of them looked eager to step any closer to the flames. John hoped the length of chain was long enough to wrap around the chicken coop and attach to the other side of the yoke.

Darting back to where he started, John picked up the other end of the chain. He eyed the gap between the chicken coop and Pierre's cabin — it was narrow, trapping the heat like an oven. Suddenly, a watery downpour crashed down on him, drenching him from head to toe. He turned around and saw Pierre, standing with an empty bucket in his hands.

"I see what you're thinking — thought I'd help," he said. "Now go do your thing."

John tightened his grip on the chain and ran for the gap. The chain clinked behind him as the coils unwound. He took a deep breath and covered his eyes.

*Out of the fire pit and into the pressure cooker,* he thought.

The water evaporated from his skin. The heat scorched his hair. He slammed his shoulder against the cabin, trying to avoid the inescapable flames surrounding him.

He opened his mouth to breathe — big mistake. Ash singed his throat; superheated smoke filled his lungs. His insides burned; tears welled up in his eyes. With a choking cough, he stumbled a few final steps forward and fell to his knees.

And the heat was gone — he'd made it through the gap! He opened his eyes and hacked the gritty air out of his lungs. Inhaling deeply, he looked at his hand. The chain was still there.

*That was easy*, he thought as he stood up. Looking over to Pierre, he noticed that he had an audience of villagers, all agog to see his next move.

*I can't let them down now.* He lowered the chain, securing it in the space between the chicken coop and the ground, flush against the joint where the stilts met the bottom of the coop. If he latched the other end of his chain to the yoke, the tvapas could pull the structure over.

He dashed toward the tvapas. The chain links thumped against the rear of the wooden coop. Just a few more steps ...

Without warning, his arm snapped back, jerking his body with it — he was out of chain. The fingers on his other hand could almost touch the tvapas.

*Hammersnap! I'm almost there!* he thought. *If those frankenmeese would take a step or two back, I could hitch them and complete the circuit.*

The tvapas continued to shy away from the flames, oblivious to his dilemma.

John gave his end of the chain a tug, hoping the tvapas would get the hint and take a step backward. No dice — apparently they didn't do "reverse." *What are my options?* he wondered. If the tvapas wouldn't step any closer to the flames ...

He looked at his left arm. How much force could it muster? *Time to find out.* He secured the chain in his left hand and extended his arm behind himself, setting his feet by digging his heels into the dirt.

Then he pulled.

"AAAAAAARRRRGGHH!" he screamed. His heart raced. Sweat exploded from every pore. His feet bored into the ground, anchoring the force of his pull.

The tvapas stumbled backward from the unexpected surge of power tugging on their yoke, then regained their footing and plowed forward to fight against it. A sharp crack rang out from behind.

John kept pulling. He couldn't feel his limbs. His vision grew blurry. Vomit rushed up from his stomach, burning his throat with acid.

Then he collapsed onto the grass and his vision went dark.

# Chapter 11

EMIKO SAT, bound to her chair by leather straps. Dust particles floated around the room like baby fireflies, dancing in the moonlight that beamed in through the window. She sneezed, causing the specks of dust to scatter violently before returning to their aimless hovering. The dry air irritated her sinuses — she couldn't bear being shut in much longer.

Her stomach growled. Every time her captors tried to spoon feed her, she spit it back out. If they wanted her to eat, they could untie her first. They were probably afraid she'd escape, or grab her gun and retaliate. She'd never shot a person until Barry, but they didn't know that. She felt no remorse, and now that she'd done it once she could do it again. Next time she wouldn't aim for the leg.

Why were they keeping her here, anyway? She tugged at her restraints, yet they refused to budge.

Just then, two shadows passed the window. Emiko stopped struggling and listened intently.

"What we gonna do with the girl?" It was Dwayne, the man who'd knocked her in the head — she recognized his voice.

"Dunno," said Jeremiah.

"Well, I was thinkin', I never had me an 'oriental' woman before ..."

*Gross!* Emiko grimaced. Another silhouette hobbled past the window — Barry, on a pair of makeshift crutches.

"That's 'cause the only woman you've had is your own sister," he said with a guffaw. Emiko heard a thumping noise — Barry smacking Dwayne with a crutch? She wondered if Barry, Jeremiah, and Dwayne had ever considered forming a traveling comedy troupe. They were more suited to slapstick than soldiering.

"Ya know that ain't true, Barry!" Dwayne said. "Why, I had me plenty of —"

"You can't have her," Barry cut in, "cause soldier boy wouldn't like it."

*Soldier boy* — it was what they called the fourth man, Private Brushnell, behind his back. Emiko hadn't seen him, but she'd heard him speak. He sounded more intelligent — and likely more dangerous — than the other three. His voice vaguely reminded her of someone, though she couldn't place it.

"Reckon this 'Osborne' guy is gonna come?" Jeremiah drawled.

"If he don't, I got first dibs on the girl," Dwayne said.

"Dwayne, I'll tell you what," Barry said. "After we reclaim Minnesota, I'll line up ten virgins and you can have first pick. I'll even throw in an Asian or two."

"What'll Brushnell say?" Dwayne asked.

"Soldier boy will be too busy kissin' the General's behind to say anything," Barry said.

The trio chuckled.

"You got yerself a deal," Dwayne said.

Emiko shook her head. Just listening to these creeps would kill her before starvation could.

"I see you're still awake," a voice said from behind her. Emiko twisted her neck to see the speaker, but he was in her blind spot. If only she were an owl ...

"How long have you been here?" she asked.

"Long enough," the voice replied. "I thought I should inform you that this will all be over tomorrow. We're going to let you go."

"What a load of moose crap," she said.

"Just as feisty as always, I see," the voice said. "Emiko."

A chill ran down Emiko's spine. She'd never told them her name.

"My brother won't let you get away with this!" she said.

"Nathan?" the voice said with a scoff. "Done watering the crops with his tears, is he?"

Emiko didn't reply … *could it be him?* she wondered.

"That's right, Emiko — I know who you are," he said. "And there's something I need you to do for me: tell Pierre and everybody else in Frontier View that I'm doing just fine without them."

"*Ramses? You're* behind this?" Emiko said.

*Ramses Brushnell!* How hadn't she recognized the voice earlier? She realized she hadn't heard his surname, Brushnell, in years — everybody in town had just called him "Ramses."

"Just deliver the message," Ramses said. Emiko heard his footsteps, leaving the room.

"I'd rather put a bullet through your brain," she said, thrashing at the leather straps.

Ramses snorted. "Always barking, but where's the bite?" he asked, as he stepped out and latched the door shut.

Emiko's blood boiled with anger. *Calm down, Emiko. Save it for tomorrow,* she thought. If Ramses was to be believed, her chance would come then, when this mysterious Osborne arrived. She took a deep breath and focused on getting a wink of sleep.

# Chapter 12

JOHN OPENED his eyes and gazed up at the hazy starlit sky. Bristles of grass massaged the skin between his fingers.

"Well," a woman's voice boomed, "look who just woke up!" She leaned over him. To his blurry vision, she looked like a bouncer — bulky and imposing. Standing up straight, she cupped her hands around her mouth and shouted, "Cynth, get over here!"

"Be right there, Doris," a voice in the distance called back.

The woman — Doris — looked back down at him.

"Pretty nuts, what you did over there," she said. "Your feet dug nearly a half foot deep into the ground."

Pushing his palms against the ground for leverage, John sat up. He looked over to this right. The smoldering chicken coop was there, resting on its side. The fire hadn't yet burnt out completely, but the remains were far enough away to no longer threaten Pierre's cabin.

"We all thought you were gonna order the tvapas to back up a step or two. You know, make them do the grunt work," Doris said. "But no siree, you pulled the whole damn building over by yourself. The wood snapped and splintered, and then *boom!*" She clapped for emphasis. "The entire building came crashing over."

"It was quite a show," said an approaching voice — Cynthia. She gave John a stern look. "Though I wasn't impressed by the part where you heaved your guts out."

John shrugged. Then he opened and shut his jaw, tilted his head back and forth, and stretched to make sure everything felt alright.

"You ladies know who started the fire?" he asked.

Doris jumped at the opportunity to answer. "Oh, I'll tell you who! It was that Ramses boy. I'm sure of it. We thought he was gone for good, but he just keeps coming back to slather it on."

"Ramses? Give me a break," Cynthia said. "That kid probably got himself eaten by a bear three steps outta town. What makes you think he'd do this?"

Doris stuck out her chin and put her hand on her hips, giving them a little wiggle.

"I can feel it in my bones," she said, beaming with pride.

With a snort, Cynthia crossed her arms and doubled over, visibly restraining herself from bursting into laughter.

"You and your bones," she said. "Is this like the time your dog disappeared and you thought a wolf had gotten him? Turned out he'd just decided life was better at the Jensen's house." She wiped away a tear. "Or that other time, when —"

"Who is Ramses?" John asked, cutting her off.

Doris straightened and prepared to answer, when another voice chimed in.

"Ramses left, oh, about ten months back," the familiar voice said. "Ambitious — overly so, I'd say. Thought he could do better out on his own."

John looked toward the voice. It was Pierre, approaching the group.

"I'm with Cynthia on this one," Pierre continued. "Nobody has caught even a whiff of him since he left. Frankly, unless he joined another community, I'd be surprised if he made it through the winter." He paused for a moment, shaking his head. "Smart kid, just too big for his britches."

John looked up at Pierre. It struck him that he was sitting on the ground, like a kid with three adults hovering around. As he pulled back a leg and started pushing himself up, Cynthia held her hand against his shoulder to restrain him.

"Whoa there, cowboy! Where do you think you're going?" she said.

Ignoring her question, John shrugged off her hand and stood up.

"Cowboy, huh?" John said, grinning as he mulled over the word. "Well, you should know — a cowboy's work is never done."

"You're still going to go to Sawbill Lake tomorrow?" Pierre asked.

"I said I would, and I do what I say — always," John replied.

Pierre smiled gently. The old man's body looked tired from the night's events, but his eyes glistened with renewed vigor.

"After seeing what you did tonight ... well, I'm sure you won't let us down," he said, giving John a big wink. "Make sure to take good care of Nathan."

"Sure thing," John said.

"Sawbill Lake? What's he gonna do at Sawbill Lake?" Doris asked.

"Doris, Pierre — could I have a moment with my patient?" Cynthia said.

"Hey, why is he going to Sawbill Lake? I wanna know," Doris said in protest.

Pierre gently reached for her arm. "I'll explain *everything*," he said, leading her away.

Cynthia looked at John sternly. "How do I know you aren't gonna pass out again tomorrow, right when the kidnappers start shooting at you? I didn't spend half a week fixing you up just to send you back into danger."

John shrugged.

"I have a job to do," he said. "Danger comes with the territory."

"I get that, but aren't you being reckless?" Cynthia said, putting her hands on the waist of her thin dress. For the first time, John noticed how slender she was.

"How does that arm of yours work, anyhow?" she asked.

"I don't know," John muttered through his beard.

"You don't know?" she asked. "I just saw you rip down a chicken coop and you tell me you don't know how you did it?"

John scowled. "You wanna know what I know?" he snarled. "I know I lost my arm in combat, and when I woke up, I found this godforsaken piece of techno-crap attached to my shoulder!" He shook his left arm in the air.

Cynthia frowned — then she slapped him across the cheek.

"We've *all* lost things — husbands, wives, children, friends — and you're sulking because you lost your arm? Not to mention got a replacement that just saved our village from burning down," she said, looking him straight in the eye. "Be grateful for what you have, John."

John stood mute, watching her blue dress flutter as she turned to walk away. What had he done to deserve *that*? He rubbed at his cheek. He imagined he'd have had a red mark if it weren't for his beard. Shaking his head, he started back toward his tent.

# Chapter 13

NATHAN AMBLED from his house to the Frontier View Co-op, guiding one of Cynthia's tvapas — a brown one with white speckles. The early morning light poured into his eyes, obscured only by the wispy clouds that crawled across the azure sky. It was perfect weather for traveling.

The single tvapa pulled a cart that Nathan had borrowed from Cynthia. It had waist high wooden wheels on either side of a square platform that his canoe rested on. Ropes held the canoe to the cart, fastened with trucker's hitches to metal brackets on either side of the platform. Two telescoping beams extended from the cart, serving as its tongue. Nathan had adjusted them so the bow and stern of the canoe would balance evenly over the cart. Leather straps affixed to the tongue were tied around the neck and back of Cynthia's tvapa. It was possible to jury-rig the cart so that multiple tvapas could pull it, but one pack animal would suffice for transporting a canoe to Sawbill Lake.

The canoe itself had long since lost its metallic shine. The aluminum body had a dull matte texture, thanks to scrapes and dents accumulated over time. Despite its appearance, Nathan imagined the canoe would serve him for many years to come — it would take a high impact puncture to breach the hull.

He had placed the canoe keel side down so that he could place gear inside — paddles, the map, his Remington 870, and a blue backpack full of odds and ends.

The sun was just peeking out from above the trees as he arrived at the Co-op — right on time. Yet John was nowhere to be found. *Strange*, he thought. He'd expected that the bearded man would arrive first.

As he waited, the Co-op's manager, Tom — a lanky, middle-aged man wearing a beige cowboy hat — strolled in, whistling as he rounded the corner of the building. He selected one of the many keys on his key ring and inserted it in the Co-op's blue door. He smiled at Nathan, greeting him with an upward nod.

"Hey there, Nathan — heading to Sawbill Lake I hear?" he said, turning the key in the lock.

"That's right," Nathan answered, surprised that Tom had heard the news.

"With that bearded guy, right?" Tom said. "He's really something else."

"He is?" Nathan asked.

"Anyway, I wouldn't want to hold you up," Tom said, taking one step inside the store. "Just let me know if you need anything." With a wave and a smile, he stepped inside and closed the wooden door.

*What is he talking about?* Nathan wondered as he stared at the door. Had Pierre gossiped to the whole town about the ransom note?

"Good morning, kid," said a voice from behind. Nathan spun around and saw John. The bearded man was wearing the same dark blue flannel shirt and jeans he'd had on the day before, along with a bulky green pack on his back.

"Why're you late?" asked Nathan.

John raised an eyebrow, then went to the canoe and swung his pack into the center of the boat.

"You're a heavy sleeper, aren't you?" he said.

"Am I?" Nathan asked, tilting his head to one side as he pondered the question. He didn't see the connection, though he was known to fall into a long slumber from time to time — Emiko called it "hibernation."

"You'll see," John said. His lips curved up into a sly grin and his eyes twinkled playfully. "I trust that you packed the things we talked about?"

"You bet," Nathan said, giving a single, affirming nod.

"Then let's go," said John. "You lead the way."

Nathan tugged at the rope attached to the tvapa's muzzle, and the heavy beast jerked its antlered head upward, lumbering forward one hoof at a time. Tvapas were slow but steady — assuming no setbacks, they'd arrive at Sawbill Lake in four or five hours.

John trotted to catch up with Nathan, meeting his stride and walking slightly behind. The pair walked past the rows of cabins as they went on their way to the trail out of town. As they approached Pierre's cabin, John pointed over to his right.

"Take a look back there," he said.

Nothing looked unusual, until Nathan noticed the burnt grass and the charred remains of Pierre's chicken coop behind the cabin. He blinked a few times in disbelief before accepting what his eyes saw.

"What happened?" Nathan asked.

"Patience, kid," John said. "It'll be a good story for the road."

\* \* \*

Nathan and John followed the wide, unpaved road northward. A light wind blew through spruce and birch trees that hung overhead, as their boots trampled the weeds that had encroached upon the gravel path. Prior to the Desolation, the road would have been populated with travelers at this time of year — people heading up to the Boundary Waters Canoe Area for a chance to get away from civilization. Now it served as a reminder of a bygone era, a time when there was actually a world to escape from.

Every so often they would pass a sign proudly declaring the area a WILDERNESS, in bold uppercase letters. Nathan understood the concept of "wilderness" — he'd grown up in the Twin Cities, a metropolitan area that had been inhabited by millions, until he was eight — and yet the signs struck him as other-worldly, like part of a cruel, twisted joke. The Boundary Waters remained unchanged, but the wilderness now extended to his front door.

After they had put some distance between themselves and Frontier View, John told Nathan about his chicken coop adventure. The roaring heat, the townspeople throwing buckets of water at it, and then how he brought it all crashing down. John seemed to enjoy sharing the tale, speaking at length without any encouragement from Nathan.

After John finished, he didn't utter another word for an hour or two. The silence broke when John stopped in his tracks and gazed up at the lush greenery overhead, spying something imperceptible to Nathan. He pulled out his revolver, aimed carefully with both hands, then cocked and fired. After the shot rang out, he cut through the trees and underbrush to look for his prize. When he reappeared, he was carrying a squirrel by the tail.

"Lunch," he said with a smirk as he threw the carcass in the canoe. A short while later he repeated the feat, bringing back a second squirrel. After he tossed it into the canoe, he spun the revolver around his finger, then held it in his palm to show Nathan.

"This is a Colt Single Action Army — the Peacemaker," said John, flicking the cylinder into a wild spin. "Chambers six bullets, but unless you're in the heat of combat, you only put in five. There's no safety, so if you keep a bullet in the top chamber, it's liable to shoot you in the leg as you're walking around."

He handed the butt of the revolver to Nathan.

Nathan examined the ivory on the grip and the silvery barrel — well-worn and dull, just like his aluminum canoe. The gun felt light in his hand, belying its imposing appearance.

"Where did you get it?" Nathan asked.

"I found it a couple years ago in an abandoned home, while I was wandering through Quebec. Been at my hip ever since," John said, patting at his empty holster. "It doesn't shoot the fastest or have the truest aim, but it's reliable — even in the rain and snow — and easy to maintain."

Nathan returned the revolver to John, who promptly returned it to its holster. Somehow, he'd expected a longer history between the man and his weapon.

"Why were you in Quebec?" he asked.

"Because I wanted to get out of Maine," John replied.

Nathan waited a moment for John to say more, but the bearded man didn't elaborate. The pair continued walking northward in silence, the summer buzz of the forest serving as their soundtrack.

* * *

The sun was at its apex when John and Nathan arrived at the south end of Sawbill Lake. John gazed out at the calm expanse of water. It was a windless day and the sun reflected clearly off the lake's smooth surface. He watched as Nathan unhitched the tvapa from the cart and tied it up to the trunk of a sturdy white pine. Meanwhile, John fetched his knife from his backpack.

"I'll prepare the meat. Could you grab some sticks and start a fire?" he asked.

"You're not worried about the smoke? Won't the kidnappers know we're here?" asked Nathan.

"Doesn't matter — they'll be expecting us, anyway," John said.

Nathan shrugged. "Alright."

John looked on as the kid wandered off into the woods, then he began skinning one of the squirrels. He started by laying it on the ground and slicing its belly open. As his hands worked, his thoughts turned elsewhere.

The kid had made for a solid partner so far. Nathan asked good questions, listened well, and didn't give John any grief. Still, the real test would come when they neared the kidnappers' outpost. Would Nathan be able to maintain his cool then?

John set his knife aside, ripped the entrails out of the squirrel — careful not to squeeze the bladder, as that could ruin the meat — and tossed them in the lake. *Better the lake than the woods*, he thought — less likely to attract bears, not to mention wolves and bobcats.

He picked up his knife and cut off the squirrel's head, limbs, and tail in quick succession. Then he flipped it over again and made an incision across the rodent's back, allowing him to peel off the skin. After setting it down, he repeated the process on the other squirrel.

Nathan returned with a bundle of sticks, which he arranged in a teepee shape in order to create a cooking fire.

Once John finished filleting the second squirrel, he rinsed the chunks of meat in the lake then placed them in the bow of the canoe. The fire would take a while to become hot, so in the meantime he went to find a couple thin sticks with which to skewer the squirrel meat. When he returned, Nathan had the fire at a steady burn. After roasting their squirrels over the fire, John and Nathan tore into the tender, nutty meat.

John finished first and tossed his skewer stick into the small fire.

"Alright kid, finish up, then we'll do some planning and recon," he said.

Nathan took one last bite, then wiped his mouth with his wrist. He grabbed the map and unfolded it on the ground in front of John.

"These are all the lakes in the area," Nathan said, pointing to a blue area on the map. "We're here — Sawbill Lake. Frontier View is down here." He dragged his finger south until it reached the edge of the map.

"Frontier View's not on the map?" John asked.

"This map was printed before the Desolation," Nathan replied. "Though Frontier View would fall to the south of it anyway."

*Sounds like the kid knows his stuff,* John thought. "Alright, where is their outpost?" he asked.

"It's not marked on the map either. The note said on the north end, right?" Nathan said, tracing his finger up the long, narrow lake. At the top, it forked east and west into two small bays. "It could be at either one of these locations," he said with a frown.

"What's this red line?" John asked, pointing at a line extending from the northeast bay.

"It's a portage," Nathan replied.

"A portage?" John asked.

"Yeah, it's what they call the trails that connect lakes together," Nathan answered. "Many date from the French and British fur trapping days."

"I imagine the outpost would be there — easier access," John said.

Nathan pointed to the northwest bay, which lacked any defining marks. "Not here?" he asked.

John took a moment to consider — was there any way to determine the outpost's location? No, not with any certainty — their plan would have to be flexible. He carefully eyed the map one more time.

"Here's the plan," he said, pointing to an island in the center of the lake, nearly as wide as the lake itself. "We'll paddle up to this island and use it as cover. As long as we're behind it, anybody on the north end of the lake won't be able to see us."

"What if they have a sentry on the island?" Nathan asked.

"I'm assuming we're dealing with a fairly small crew. A large group of crooks wouldn't bother with kidnapping — too much effort for a non-guaranteed payday. Get more than a handful of men together and you're better off robbing a bank," John said.

"So?" Nathan said.

"So, let's say they have four or five men. I doubt they'll have a sentry posted, but if they do it's to our advantage — we can deal with him before we reach the main group. And if they do have more than a handful of men stationed here, with ample manpower to secure the island and the north outpost ... well, we're going to be in trouble regardless."

Nathan gulped and nodded. "Got it."

John continued, returning his attention to the map. "Moving along — at the island's tip, we'll split up. You'll continue north in the canoe." He dragged his finger straight north. "Meanwhile," he said, returning his finger to the mainland adjacent to the island. "I'll bushwhack over ground and flank the outpost." He traced a land route, starting from the shore to the right of the island, all the way up to the north end.

"They could be in either one of these northern bays," he continued. "If I arrive before you, it's not a problem — I can hide in the woods. That's a luxury you won't have. You can't hesitate once they spot you."

"So, what do we do?" Nathan asked.

"You'll give me a thirty-minute head start. That should give me enough time to reach either bay," John said.

Nathan nodded. "Okay, then what?" he asked.

John walked over to the canoe to pick up Nathan's blue pack. "See this bag?" he said.

"Yeah, I'm not blind," Nathan said.

"It's full of money." John gave the bag a stern pat.

"It is?"

"No, but if you want the kidnappers to believe it, you'd better convince yourself it is," John replied.

"But won't they find it suspicious that we could round up $5,000 on such short notice?" Nathan pointed out.

John's lips curled into a wry grin. "Who said anything about $5,000?"

# Chapter 14

NATHAN SAT quietly in the stern of the canoe, rhythmically slicing the water with his lacquered spruce paddle. Its bent shaft offered an improved angle and increased leverage over ordinary straight shaft paddles. The canoe cut through the water gracefully, leaving only a gently curling wake. Trees surrounded the lake on every side, the reflections of their jagged green peaks clinging to the shallow waters along the shoreline.

A wispy, high-pitched bird call cut through the air. Nathan looked up — above John's head, a bald eagle soared high in the sky. It swooped downward, vigorously flapping its thick, dark brown wings. As it neared the surface of the water, it spread its wings wide and kicked its feet forward. The eagle swung its talons downward into the lake and snatched a fish, splashing the water with the tips of its wings as it carried its catch upward, eventually disappearing into the trees.

"Makes me wish I could fly," Nathan said.

"Switch," John called out, ignoring the comment. He shifted his paddle from the boat's left side to the right; Nathan did the opposite.

The island approached on their left. Once they passed it, their canoe would be visible to anyone standing in the northwestern bay. They guided the canoe along its shore, gliding to a rest at the easternmost edge of the south side.

"Let's make this quick," John said.

With swift strokes, they paddled from the island to the shore, careful to minimize any chance of being seen from the north. John lifted his paddle from the water and rocks grated at the bottom of the canoe as they ran aground to let him out. Nathan watched as John hopped out onto the rocky shore. The bearded man gently placed his paddle back in the canoe and checked that his revolver was in its holster.

"See you on the other side, kid," he said, winking at Nathan before darting off into the woods. Nathan looked on as John's blue flannel shirt became harder and harder to pick out, until finally the bearded man disappeared behind the cover of the tree trunks.

And now to wait. Nathan looked up toward the sky and let the gentle rippling of the waves soothe his ears. Realizing there was no reason to wait in the canoe, he crawled to the front and stepped out, eventually finding a comfortable resting spot in the grass along the shore.

How had it all come to this — paddling across a lake to rescue his sister from kidnappers, in the middle of nowhere, armed with only a shotgun? A scant ten years ago, the police would've handled any hostage situation. Post-Desolation, the problem was his alone.

Nathan closed his eyes and let his mind wander, allowing it to return to that time, nearly nine years ago.

The drought ... fighting all over the country ... martial law in Minneapolis ... nuclear strikes ...

At the time, he hadn't understood what was happening, and even now his understanding of those chaotic days was largely abstract, pieced together from vague youthful memories and the stories he'd heard from Pierre and his father.

His memories of the events that followed, however, were far more vivid.

Viral outbreak ... every last one friends getting sick ... his family locking themselves inside ... his mother vomiting uncontrollably as she withered away ... the palpable aura of decay that hung over Minneapolis in the aftermath ...

That was the Desolation, and Nathan, as well as his sister and father, were incredibly lucky to have survived its effects, thanks to a rare genetic immunity.

He remembered the months that followed and how fortunate he had been to have had his father watching over him and Emiko as they drifted around Minneapolis, gathering every last bit of food they could find. And he thought back to the following spring, when his family had moved north and settled in the area which he now knew as Frontier View.

Nathan's life before the Desolation hardly seemed real any more. Minneapolis was merely a distant memory; Frontier View was his home now. His father had helped him and Emiko get started in this newly desolate world, but Ryota couldn't help now. It was Nathan's time to step up.

Turning his thoughts back to the present, Nathan opened his eyes as he sat up to stretch. As he gazed out across the shimmering blue water, he noticed that his canoe was no longer resting on the shore.

It was drifting in the middle of the lake, with all of his supplies inside of it.

# Chapter 15

JOHN PASSED through the dense foliage, careful to keep the glistening blue lake within view so as not to lose his way. He was nearing the northern end of the eastern bay and had yet to see the outpost. *Must be on the western bay,* he thought. No matter — the head start Nathan gave him could accommodate an extra half-mile of bushwhacking.

Soon he'd be at the trail — the red line on the map that Nathan had called a "portage." Though he didn't have a map of his own, John had memorized all of the lake's major features during the planning session. It occurred to him that the outpost could be along the portage, rather than right on the lake — a possibility they hadn't considered in their strategy. On one hand, an outpost off the lake's shore would be better hidden. Then again, traffic in this area was sparse and the kidnappers probably would've included that detail on the ransom note. Either way, he had faith that Nathan could figure it out.

A dull, resonant hammering sound echoed in the distance — a woodpecker, knocking at a tree. John smiled as he listened. Frontier View was a nice little village, but this, the wilderness, was his true home now. Moreover, he looked forward to the task at hand. A person in need, a half-baked plan, and a partner — he was in his element and he intended to savor it.

Ahead, a rough trail came into view — the portage. Rocks littered the narrow, muddy path as it met the lake, before weaving north through the trees. Bushes and weeds crowded the edges of the portage trail — signs of disuse. Despite the overgrowth, the crude trail still made travel between lakes more convenient. Now, if only the forest rangers had cut a path *around* Sawbill Lake as well. That would have streamlined the mission.

*Still no sign of the outpost*, John noted, letting out a groan. His jaunt through the woods was taking longer than he'd expected.

A throaty snarl sounded from ahead in reply.

John looked up. From the other side of the trail, a black bear glared back at him — a mother bear standing defensively in front of her two cubs. Shiny black fur stretched across her muscular body, glistening in the sunlight. John gulped. Black bears weren't predators and generally avoided humans, but a mother protecting her cubs? Trouble.

The mother bear stood up on two feet and unleashed a guttural roar, staring at John with her beady black eyes. John froze, unflinchingly returning the bears gaze. He felt the grip of the Colt in his holster ... no, he couldn't shoot the bear. The sound of gunfire would alert the kidnappers of his presence.

The bear fell back down on all fours and slowly approached John, moving surefootedly with swaying hips. She let out a vicious growl, making it clear that she didn't want John anywhere near her two cubs.

Adrenaline rushed through John's body. Fighting was an option. Though the odds wouldn't be in his favor, he could try to use his bionic arm to fend off the beast.

But that would take time. John didn't have time — Nathan was probably already waiting. *Maybe next time, mama bear,* he thought. Then he broke into a mad dash, cutting to the left of the burly bear and making a break for the woods on the other side of the trail. The mother bear swiveled and turned to cut off his escape. Her paws thumped against the forest floor as her slow walk became a thundering stride, with all four feet leaving the ground simultaneously as she bounded toward John.

The bear drew close and lunged at John's right side, batting one of her massive paws at his head. John dipped to his left, ducking just underneath the powerful swipe. *Just like turning the corner on a linebacker in high school football,* he thought. And also just like in football, he wasn't gonna look back. Bobbing and weaving around the trees in his path, he sprinted toward the western bay where Nathan was surely waiting.

# Chapter 16

FACING THE STERN of the canoe and reaching an arm across to the opposite gunwale, Nathan thrust himself into the boat with a series of strong scissor kicks, followed by a quick rotation of his upper body. The canoe rocked violently back and forth as he fell into its aluminum body. As he hacked up a lungful of lake water, he chided himself for forgetting to tie down the canoe. It was a serious oversight, causing him to waste time and energy. Water streamed from his white t-shirt, dripping along the bottom of the canoe as he crawled toward the stern. He took a seat — it was paddlin' time.

His paddle cut the surface of the water, creating a vortex as he propelled the canoe forward. He repeated the process again and again, switching sides often in order to keep the bow pointed northward. The trees drifted past him on either side — the calm backdrop felt at odds with the danger that lurked ahead. He paddled faster, eager to reach the north end of the lake. The sooner he arrived, the less time he'd have to second-guess himself.

What he was doing was crazy. He felt like he was walking into a den of wolves with a life-size inflatable moose in his hands, hoping to offer it as a show of peace. Wouldn't the kidnappers see through his bluff right away and shoot him on the spot? What if John came late? What if something happened to Emiko? What if ... no, he had to stop thinking like that. Given the circumstances, he and John had done everything they could to prepare. Now it was time to stick to the plan, come what may.

Dead ahead, he saw it — the outpost, partially hidden in the trees along the north end of the western bay. It appeared to be a single-story timber building of a fashion similar to the cabins in Frontier View. However, it was far wider — about two and a half times the width of Nathan's two room cabin. From his head-on perspective, he could only guess at how far back into the woods the outpost extended.

However, the cabin was merely a backdrop. In front of it there were three figures, their features not distinguishable from this distance. One of them was sitting in a chair — probably Emiko. The other two figures stood on either side of her, staring out across the lake. Nathan felt a chill run down his spine, knowing Emiko's captors could shoot him or sink his canoe at will. He slowed his pace, taking the opportunity to catch his breath. Since John was circling in from the east, it would take him a little longer to arrive here, at the western bay. Nathan hoped John would arrive on time, because he had little confidence in his ability to bluff for time as he waited for the bearded man's arrival.

The canoe glided across the surface of the water, like a tiny asteroid drifting through outer space, on a crash course with the moon. As he approached, the situation became clearer. Emiko was bound and gagged in a chair, about five yards from the rocky shore. A short, heavyset man stood to her left, supporting himself with a wooden crutch. To her right was a gaunt, pale-skinned man wearing a red trucker's cap. Both men carried long-barreled guns and wore thin green vests over dark shirts paired with blue jeans. Behind them stood the outpost, larger than even the Frontier View Co-op.

Emiko weakly struggled at her bonds. She appeared unharmed, but Nathan wouldn't be able to tell without talking to her. Anger rose within him — if they'd done anything to her ...

He took a deep breath to calm himself and focused on his paddling. Finally, he reached the shoreline. The aluminum hull of his canoe scraped against the pebbles littered along the shore, breaking the eerie silence.

The thin man aimed his gun directly at Nathan. It appeared to be a high-powered hunting rifle rather than a shotgun.

"Hey, Barry, didn't Brushnell say our man'd have a thick, scruffy beard?" the thin man asked.

*Brushnell? Could it be?* Nathan wondered.

"Shut it, Dwayne," the larger man — Barry — snapped. Because of the crutch supporting his right side, he couldn't properly hold his gun. His right arm hung over the crutch and he held the gun's trigger at waist level in his right hand, while supporting the long barrel with his left palm.

"Got our money, kid?" he said.

"Well, about that," Nathan said. "See, we have a small problem — I don't have $5,000." *Moose in heat, this is insane,* he thought.

Barry glared at him. "What're you trying to say?"

"You can't honestly expect a kid like me to find 5,000 bucks on such short notice. But I did my best. I can pay you 1,500 now," Nathan offered, pointing the backpack in the front of the canoe. "And I'll get you the rest by next week. With interest, of course."

"Oh yeah? How much interest you talking?" Dwayne said, eyeing Nathan down the barrel of his rifle.

Barry growled "Christ, Dwayne, why don't you let me —"

"An extra three grand," Nathan cut in. "$8,000 in total." As the words rolled off his tongue, he could practically see flakes of gold sparkling in Dwayne's eyes.

Barry, however, still appeared doubtful. "I'll tell you what," he said. "You show us the money you have and then we'll decide what to do."

Nathan frowned. "Don't trust me?" he said.

"Don't need to," Barry said with a devious grin. "Dwayne, go have a look at the bag."

The thin man nodded and then slowly crept toward Nathan's canoe, careful to keep his gun trained on Nathan.

*Moose scat!* What had gone wrong? Nathan had said everything *exactly* the way John had told him to. Next he was supposed to demand that they return his sister first — only then would he give them the money. That plan clearly wouldn't work now, but he still had to buy time until John arrived.

"So," he asked Dwayne, trying to sound nonchalant, "what are you going to do with all that money?"

Dwayne paused and smacked his lips.

"Ain't thought 'bout it much," he said, turning to his partner. "Barry, what we doin' with the money?"

"How about you make sure we actually have it first?" said Barry, glowering at Dwayne.

"Good thinkin'," Dwayne replied. He started toward the canoe again and set his eyes on the bulky green pack. "In here?" He asked, pointing with his gun.

Nathan nodded silently.

"Hey, Barry," Dwayne said. "How can I open it with this gun in my hands?"

After thinking a moment, Barry let out a frustrated sigh. "Alright, have the kid open the pack for you."

"You heard him," Dwayne said, motioning Nathan toward the pack.

*Well,* Nathan thought, a*t least this buys me a few more moments.* Cautiously, he crawled toward the bow of the canoe, stepping over his Remington 870 on the way. His instincts screamed at him to reach for the gun, to fight back, but he knew that the kidnappers would riddle him with bullets before he could even take aim. Stepping over the yoke, he continued forward and reached out to touch the backpack.

"Make it quick," Barry commanded. "No monkey business."

Nathan nodded, letting out a nervous sigh. He took one last look at Emiko. She stared back at him with apprehension in her eyes. She undoubtedly realized he didn't have $1,500. Soon the kidnappers would know too.

As he reached for the zipper, Nathan caught a glimpse of something moving on the roof of the outpost. It fell out of sight behind the slanted roof, then slowly reappeared.

*John!*

The bearded man turned his head back and forth, surveying the scene, then nodded and gave a thumbs-up signal.

Suppressing the urge to smile, Nathan looked back down at the pack. He began to unzip it, confident that with John covering the roof they were in control of the situation. The zipper purred as Nathan pulled it open.

Dwayne took his sights off Nathan's head and stuck the muzzle into the backpack, poking around to see what was inside.

"There ain't a single dollar in here!" he cried out, looking back to Barry for direction.

"Did you really think a kid could get us that kind of money? Now hurry up and shoot him. He's nothing to us," Barry snorted.

"Didn't soldier boy say not to shoot 'em?" Dwayne questioned.

"No, he said not to shoot the bearded man," Barry said. "Do you see a beard on this kid?"

Dwayne shrugged. "Good point." He pressed the muzzle of his rifle against Nathan's head.

Nathan's heart began to race. *John, what are you waiting for? Hurry up!*

"So kid," Dwayne said. "Got any last wo —"

# Chapter 17

JOHN HAD SEEN enough — he pulled the trigger. The crack of his Colt ripped through the air and a bullet slammed into the side of the thin man's head. Blood and chunks of cranium exited his exploding skull, plopping into the shallow water of the shoreline. The splash of the collapsing corpse followed.

The portly man awkwardly hopped on one leg, spinning around to look up at the roof. His crutch slipped out from his right armpit and he struggled to maintain his balance on one leg.

"You!" he exclaimed. "*You're* John Osborne!" He clumsily pointed his shotgun at John, unable to properly aim it while standing on one leg.

"That I am," John said. He raised his hands in the air, feigning surrender — he didn't know why these guys wanted him, but he knew they wanted him alive.

"Giving up easy, huh?" Barry called out.

"No, I just think my friend will have more fun dealing with you." John pointed toward the woods.

The mother black bear was creeping out from the trees, approaching Barry, Nathan, and his sister Emiko.

"What the Desolation — you brought a pet bear?" Barry screeched. He took aim at the massive black animal and fired off a volley of buckshot.

The bear wailed in pain then began charging directly at the hefty man. One poorly aimed shotgun blast from that distance wasn't going to slow her down. Bypassing Emiko, the bear roared as she lunged straight at Barry, knocking him over.

*That could've been me.* John grimaced at the thought. "Hey, kid, pick up your gun and untie your sister!" he shouted down at Nathan from the rooftop. "I'll take care of the rest."

\* \* \*

Without a word, Nathan gestured *OK* with his hand. He picked up the Remington from the bottom of the canoe then dashed over to his sister, circling behind her chair and hurriedly untying the ropes around her wrists.

"Don't worry, Emiko. Everything's gonna be alright," he said.

She let out an unintelligible reply, muffled by the gag.

To his right, Nathan heard the bear unleash an angry roar. A shotgun went off — probably Barry trying to keep it at bay.

There — his sister was free! Emiko jumped up and immediately reached behind her head to untie the white cloth around her mouth.

"Let me help you," Nathan said, pulling at the knot. The cloth came undone and fell to the ground. Emiko spit out the cotton sock that had been stuffed in her mouth.

"What took you so long!" she said.

*Good to see a few days of imprisonment haven't broken her spirit*, Nathan thought.

"Don't I get a thank you?" he asked.

Without replying, Emiko looked over at Barry, who was pinned beneath the bear. The portly man was screaming frantically, trying to aim his shotgun as the bear battered him back and forth on the ground.

"Emiko — how many kidnappers were there?" Nathan said, trying to regain her attention.

"How many — ah, four, I think," she said.

"Four?"

"Yeah, and one of them ..." She trailed off mid-sentence, shifting her gaze back toward the outpost. "They have dad's gun inside!" she blurted out. Without giving Nathan a chance to reply, she tore off toward the door of the outpost.

"Emiko!" he shouted after her. What the Desolation was she thinking! She opened the outpost door and disappeared inside. With a reluctant sigh, Nathan tightened his grip around the shotgun and followed her in.

* * *

Scouting the area for other kidnappers, John trotted to the far end of the roof. As he approached the ledge, a shotgun boomed from below. He grimaced and dropped the Colt as a wild surge of pain rushed through his right arm. The Colt hit the roof and slid toward the eaves before falling out of sight. *I thought they had orders not to shoot at me.* Apparently this guy didn't get the memo.

No gun — what could he do? He dropped to one knee and with his left hand he ripped one of the thick spruce shingles from the roof. With the heavy shingle in hand, he rolled backward, putting distance between himself and his attacker. Then he stood up and began running for the edge of the roof, wincing in pain as his right arm swung back and forth. The gunner below shot at him again — a miss.

John reached the ledge and jumped. He could see his assailant now — a dark-skinned man, wearing a green vest. As John flew overhead, the man followed with his shotgun and fired a volley into the air — but missed.

John hit the ground, rolling forward to reduce the shock of impact. He stood up and turned around.

"You're John Osborne?" the man asked, pointing his shotgun straight at John.

John scowled, growling through his beard in reply. Then he raised his left arm overhead, and with a guttural roar he heaved the wooden shingle like a throwing axe. The dark-skinned man's eyes opened wide in fear as the shingle spun forward through the air. Then it tore into the man's throat, and his body went limp, crumpling to the grass.

All was quiet. John looked more closely at his right arm. Two shotgun pellets had burrowed deep inside his forearm — there was nothing he could do about that right now. Cautiously, he walked back around to the front of the outpost.

The bear was there. Or its remains were, anyway. It was a bloody, mangy, mass of black fur, lying prone. John walked up to it and saw the fat man with the broken leg, pinned underneath the massive corpse. His eyes were closed; blood and bruises marked his face, but he was still breathing.

John stood over the man, looking down at his face. "Mama bear caught you with your hand in the honey jar, didn't she?" he said.

The man weakly opened his eyes and stared up at John.

"Who ... what the hell are you?" he said, his voice a rasping whisper.

John walked away without replying and retrieved his Colt from where it had hit the ground. Nathan and Emiko had disappeared — they must've run inside. Spinning the cylinder of his revolver to a live round, he approached the open door of the outpost.

# Chapter 18

STEPPING LIGHTLY, Nathan crept through the outpost's narrow hallway. Doors on either side opened to a handful of small rooms — Emiko had to be in one of them. Why was his sister so childish? What was she thinking, running back into the outpost to fetch her Ruger? Nathan didn't care that it was their father's — he just wanted to get everyone in the canoe and make a break for safety.

He put his hand on a door to the right. Its hinges creaked as he swung it open. With the stock of his Remington tight against his shoulder, he sidestepped in front of the open door, only to find that the room was completely empty. *I almost feel like a real soldier*, he thought.

*Was there always an outpost here?* he wondered. He didn't come to Sawbill Lake often, so he couldn't say for sure. Whoever built the structure had designed it with ample room for storing weapons and people.

The cluck of a chicken broke the eerie silence. *One of Pierre's?* Nathan couldn't tell exactly where the sound had come from, but he didn't have time to look for it now.

He stepped back into the main hallway — one door remained, on his left. It was already open. Silently, he rested his back against the wall next to it and readied his shotgun. Then he spun into the doorframe.

In the middle of the small room was his sister. A man stood behind her, with his hand over her mouth and a pistol to her head. She let out a muffled cry.

"Ramses!" Nathan shouted. "Let her go!" His fingers tightened around his gun, though he didn't have a good shot. The room was sparsely furnished. A desk sat against one wall, bare except for a glass window. The only other notable feature was the rear door, likely leading outside — Ramses' escape plan.

"Nathan? What a pleasant surprise," Ramses said. "I didn't know you had it in you."

Nathan narrowed his eyes. "You left Frontier View to become a kidnapper?" he asked.

"No — I left that little Podunk town so I could change the world," Ramses said. "The people need a leader, Nathan. We can't live like savages forever."

*Who gave him that idea?* The Ramses Nathan remembered was a village bully, not a world-changing visionary.

"I don't have your money," he said. He could feel the sweat gathering in his palms — he'd never experienced tension like this before. Emiko's eyes were pleading with him to act, but he didn't see anything he could do. His shotgun wasn't a precision tool. Even if he aimed directly between Ramses' eyes, the spread would hit Emiko as well.

Ramses snorted. "This was never about the money," he said. "I just need you to do a favor for me."

"How about I give you a mouthful of lead?" Nathan said, surprised at his own aggressiveness.

"Sounds like you've learned a thing or two from our friend John," Ramses said. "Speaking of whom, I have a message for him."

"You kidnapped Emiko to get to him?" Nathan said with rising anger. "That was your motive?"

Ramses didn't respond. He stepped back toward the door, dragging Emiko with him.

"I was hoping I could deliver the message to him in person, but you —" He stopped short, shifting his gaze beyond Nathan. "Ah, and there he is! John Osborne himself," he said. "Did my compatriots outside treat you well?"

"About as well as a guy like me could expect, showing up unannounced. They welcomed me with hot lead, so I returned the favor," John's voice said — Nathan didn't dare turn to look back at him.

Ramses' eyes grew wide. He didn't reply, except to take another step back toward the door. His hand was still clasped tightly around Emiko's mouth.

"Let her go," John said. Nathan heard the click of John cocking his revolver.

"I have something to tell you first," Ramses said. His voice had lost its tinge of arrogance.

"I couldn't give a rat's —"

"About your arm," Ramses said, cutting John short.

The room fell silent.

"Listen carefully, because I won't repeat myself. The man who designed your arm — you can find him on Mallard Island, located to the north, on Rainy Lake," Ramses said.

"Who are you?" John barked, losing his cool for the first time since Nathan had met him.

"A friend of law and order," Ramses said, with no hint of irony. "The question, John, is: Who are *you*?" With that, he gave Emiko a hard shove forward and ducked behind her. He forced the back door open with his shoulder and dashed out into the wilderness.

Nathan lowered his gun and let out a sigh of relief.

John rushed past Nathan, heading for the door. His eyes flared with passion — he looked dead set on chasing Ramses. However, he stopped and looked down at Emiko. She'd fallen on her knees, exhausted. John gave the back door another passing glance, then knelt beside her.

"You okay, kid?" he asked.

Emiko didn't reply. Her long black hair hung down over her eyes, hiding her face as she let out a sob.

Nathan rushed to her, setting his gun down on the desk. He fell to his knees and threw his arms around Emiko.

"Loons over the moon, Emiko! What were you thinking, running back in here?" he asked.

"I ... I don't know," Emiko said between choking sobs. "I couldn't let them have my gun ... dad's gun."

"Hey, it's okay," Nathan said, giving her a reassuring squeeze. "We can go back home now."

She sniffled in reply. Nathan pulled away from her and examined her face. "Did they do anything to you?" he asked.

Her long hair waved back and forth as she shook her head, before meeting eyes with Nathan.

"What is Beard doing here?" she asked.

"Beard?" John sneered in disgust.

"He's a friend," Nathan said, turning to look at the bearded man with a proud smile. "I couldn't have rescued you without him."

Rising to his feet, John pursed his lips and shook his head.

"What's wrong?" Nathan asked.

"Something ain't right," John muttered. "That kid knew too much about me."

"Ramses?" Nathan said. "He used to live in Frontier View. What's he care about your —" He stopped mid-sentence, as his eyes caught a glimpse of the red droplets streaking down John's arm. "What happened to your arm?" he asked.

"What, this?" John said, grimacing in pain as he tried to raise his right arm. "Nothing a little bit of Cynthia's soup won't fix." He walked over and leaned against the desk.

*Moose pie!* thought Nathan. How were they going to get home in this condition? He just hoped none of Barry's shotgun blasts had punctured the canoe.

"Can we go now?" Emiko whined.

With a groan, John stood up straight from the desk.

"She's right — we should go. That frankenmoose won't wait all day," he said.

"Frankenmoose?" Emiko snorted.

"He means a tvapa," Nathan said.

"Whatever. Either way it's a freak on a yoke," John said.

The trio began heading back through the outpost toward the entrance. A chicken clucked somewhere in the distance.

"We should probably do something about the chickens," Nathan said. "I have a feeling they're Pierre's."

"Well, we can't bring them back with us," John said.

Emiko smiled. "Then let's set them free."

"Sounds good to me," Nathan said, shifting his attention to John. "By the way, can you paddle with your arm in that condition?" He still wanted to know what Ramses meant ... how could someone *design* John's arm?

"Can a woodchuck chuck wood?" John said.

Nathan replied, "You know, woodchucks actually can't —"

"I know. Let's go," John said as he stepped outside.

* * *

Emiko sat on a log, listening to the crackling of the campfire as she gazed into the hypnotic orange and red embers. The group had set up camp at the south end of Sawbill Lake, as it was too late to head back to Frontier View that night. She cradled the Ruger 10/22 in her arms, like it was a part of her. She didn't ever want to part with it again.

Discreetly, she shifted her eyes to look at John. He was ripping off a strip of his plaid shirt to bandage his wounded right arm. Her eyes turned to his left arm. It looked like ... well, it looked like an ordinary arm.

After much prying on Nathan's part, John had finally divulged what little he knew about his arm. He'd lost his real arm in combat, *before* the Desolation. Then he'd fallen into a coma, and awakened *after* the Desolation with a new arm attached to his shoulder. The hospital where he woke up was empty — not a single person remained, leaving him with no one to describe the nature of the new limb. He quickly discovered the bionic arm had nearly boundless strength, but beyond that he had no idea how it worked.

And now, he also wondered how Ramses knew about it. John hadn't told a soul about the arm, meaning Ramses must have heard about it from someone who knew more. John was determined to find out whom that someone was.

Continuing to mull over John's dilemma, Emiko turned to look at Nathan, who was snoring as usual. She'd never seen him act so bravely. Where he had gotten the courage from she couldn't say.

Contentedly, she looked up at the stars and picked out the constellations her dad had taught her — Andromeda, Hercules, Ursa Major. Their twinkling glow was reflected in her eyes.

Emiko smiled. *Nathan, I knew you'd come for me*, she thought to herself.

With a yawn, she again stared at the flickering embers of the campfire. As much as she loved the wilderness, right now she wanted nothing more than to wake up early tomorrow and return to Frontier View.

# Chapter 19

THE DULL TWANG of fingers striking rusty guitar strings carried through Loon's Landing. John stood in the back corner, alone. He lifted his glass and let the harsh scent of moonshine whiskey hit his nose before taking a quick gulp. The liquor triggered his gag reflex and he nearly spit it back up before forcing it down. *They should just call it what it is: frankenmoose piss,* he mused, setting the glass down on the nearest table.

Thankfully, the music was better than the booze. The guitarist — a young man, wearing a dark plaid shirt and a black beret — sat in another corner, strumming an old song John vaguely recognized and singing, "Don't stop believing, just hold on to that feeling." A small crowd stood around him, clapping between songs and chatting all the while.

John thought back ... how long had it been since he'd played guitar? Not since high school. He held his left arm out, examining it as he wiggled his fingers, imagining the crunch of a rosewood fretboard splintering underneath his superhuman grip.

Cynthia stood among the audience, her long white skirt swaying gently back and forth with the music. She looked back and smiled at him, then tilted her head toward the guitarist, encouraging John to join. John shook his head, then looked down at the grimy wooden floor. Despite the dim, flickering lamplight, the dust accumulation on the floor was readily visible.

"No drink for you tonight?" a voice asked.

John swung his head upward to find Pierre approaching with a beer mug in hand. The old man eyed the abandoned whiskey glass on the table.

"Maybe you should try a beer," Pierre said. "It goes down a bit easier than the whiskey."

"Yeah?" John said with a smirk as he leaned back against the wall.

"How's the arm?" Pierre asked.

John looked at his right arm, bandaged and in a sling. He thought the sling was overkill, but Cynthia insisted that he wear it for a few days.

"Just a scratch," he said. "It'll heal faster than you can rebuild your chicken coop."

"Think so?" Pierre said. "Say, did you hear the truth about the coop?"

John raised an eyebrow — last he'd heard, the villagers thought Ramses had burned it down.

"Turns out," Pierre continued, "that my neighbor's kid was playing with an old Zippo lighter inside and accidentally started a pile of wood chips on fire. Confessed to it this afternoon. He's gonna make it up to me by doing some chores and field work. Claims he wasn't the one taking the chickens though."

"I think the boys on Sawbill Lake were responsible for that," John said.

"That right? Say, wanna lead another rescue team?" Pierre said with a wink.

John groaned, shaking his head.

"Sounds like fun to me," Nathan's voice exclaimed as he strolled over to join the conversation, ceramic mug in hand.

"Aren't you too young to be drinking?" John asked.

"Oh, this?" Nathan said, raising his mug. "Just water."

"Is Emiko doing alright?" asked Pierre.

"Yeah, she's still … Emiko. Still making messes, still leaving her bed unmade, still …" Nathan trailed off with a sigh. Then he perked up and looked at John. "Say, when are we heading to Mallard Island?"

"We?" said John. He hadn't planned on bringing company.

"Won't you need a guide?" Nathan asked. "I found the island on a map — looks like it's best if we cut south through Duluth before heading north again."

"I work better alone." John said. "Besides, it's none of your business."

"Gotcha," Nathan said, slumping his shoulders and hanging his head. The three stood in silence for a moment, listening to the guitarist's heavy strumming.

"But what if you lose consciousness again?" Pierre asked John, breaking the silence.

*That's a good question,* thought John as he rubbed his bearded chin. He hadn't passed out recently, but he still didn't fully understand the nature of his blackouts.

"What do you suggest?" he asked.

Silently, Pierre tilted his head sideways, toward downtrodden Nathan.

*He wants me to bring the kid?* John wondered. Did Pierre understand the danger involved? Nathan was certainly brave — braver than he gave himself credit for — but he wasn't much of a fighter. *Then again,* John considered, *the old man told me that at the beginning, right here in this bar. Maybe he knows something I don't …*

"Alright kid," he finally said. "I'll consider it."

"Really?" Nathan's eyes lit up like two spotlights, cutting through the poorly lit tavern. "Pierre, you'll look out for Emiko?"

"Of course," Pierre said with a nod.

"Hey now, you can't pull the trigger before the hammer's cocked," warned John. "I said I'd think about it — nothing more."

"Thanks John," Nathan said with a big grin, before turning to go talk with another group of friends that had formed near the bartender's counter.

John shook his head. What had he gotten himself into?

"You'll appreciate having him along — I'm sure of it," Pierre said, patting John on the shoulder. "And I appreciate it too. Nathan needs to see that there's more to this world than just our little village."

"You're not worried about him?" John asked.

Pierre looked across the tavern at Nathan, then raised the glass of beer to his lips and took a hearty sip. "I feel the winds of change coming," he said, "and I know they'll blow into Frontier View sooner or later, no matter how much we try to keep them at bay."

"Are you talking about Ramses?" John asked.

Pierre didn't reply immediately. He took a final sip of his beer then set the glass down on a nearby table.

"No," he said. "I'm not afraid of Ramses. But I am afraid of whoever emboldened him. Nathan said Ramses was espousing the virtues of law and order. Those certainly aren't ideals he discovered on his own in the wilderness."

John shrugged. "What's wrong with a little order?"

"Nothing," Pierre said, looking John straight in the eye, "unless you're the one being ordered around."

John nodded gently in agreement with the old man. *Still, what I wanna know is: how did that punk kid know about my arm?* He hoped Mallard Island would provide the answer.

# Chapter 20

FOR TWO DAYS Ramses had run north, seeking a place to regroup after losing everything at Sawbill Lake. Though he'd been waiting inside the outpost during the battle outside, he'd seen much of the action through a window. He'd witnessed Dwayne taking a bullet through the eyes and Barry's hopeless attempt to fend off the black bear. He didn't visually confirm Jeremiah's death, yet he saw no reason to doubt Osborne's word. The bearded man was like a machine, whose gears churned out death with the force of inevitability.

And so he'd delivered his message and ran. His feet had carried him here, to the General's Gunflint Lake outpost — less than a mile south of the former Minnesota-Canadian border. The day was nearly gone and the sun slowly drifted toward the western skyline, casting brilliant hues of magenta and crimson against the peaks of the trees.

Ramses wrapped his fingers around the handle of the front door. The Gunflint Lake outpost was rather expansive. It stood two stories tall, had solar panels on its roof to provide electricity, and if Ramses' memory served correctly, it contained an expansive cache of weapons and other supplies. In the rush to escape Osborne and Nathan, he'd left his radio behind; the General would be waiting for a report.

Swinging the door open, he scanned the interior. The main room looked like a large one-room office. A handful of windows allowed the waning sunlight to illuminate the room and a half dozen desks lined the floor — makeshift workstations, with radios, pens, paper, and other office supplies strewn across their wooden surfaces. On the far side of the office was a staircase that led upstairs. This outpost was far more luxurious than the threadbare shack at Sawbill Lake.

Ramses flipped the light switch near the door. After some flickering false starts, fluorescent lamps flooded the room with artificial white light. He walked to the nearest desk. A hand drawn June calendar sat on the back corner of the desk, suggesting that the soldiers stationed at this outpost must have left last month. That would explain the fine dust covering the floor and desktops.

A faint pattering noise came from above. Ramses froze and listened carefully. The sound didn't repeat. *Probably just a squirrel running across the roof,* he thought, noting to look into it when he went upstairs. He spotted a radio on one of the other desks and stepped over to pick it up. As he began tuning it to the General's frequency, he noticed a mirror on the wall.

*I look like I faced the Desolation itself,* he thought as he gazed into the mirror. Streaks of brown mud marked his face, and his short hair was missing its usual luster. His ragged fatigues needed repair as well. He lifted one of the dark green sleeves and took a whiff of his underarm, immediately recoiling in disgust. Unfortunately, a bath would have to wait. He turned on the radio and relayed his message.

"This is Private Brushnell, reporting from Gunflint Lake outpost."

A faint voice replied through the speaker. Ramses held the radio close to his ear — the volume control wasn't functioning properly.

"Could you repeat that?" Ramses said.

"Hello, Private Brushnell — the General has been waiting for your report. I'll patch you through to him."

"Thank you."

Ramses waited a moment.

"This is the General."

"Private Brushnell speaking, sir. Reporting from Gunflint Lake outpost."

"I was worried we'd lost you, son."

"We suffered three casualties, sir. I'm the only survivor."

The General paused, as though observing a moment of silence.

"I'm sorry to hear that, son. What of the mission?"

"I communicated the information to Osborne, sir. He sounded *very* interested — I imagine he'll head to Mallard Island soon."

"And you didn't mention me?"

"That's correct, sir."

"You've done well, son. To stand against John Osborne and survive is no small feat. I want you to report back to HQ as soon as possible for a full debriefing. From there, we can determine what our next step will be."

"And what of Osborne, sir?"

"That's no longer your concern."

Ramses paused, frowning momentarily.

"You hear me, Private?"

"Understood, sir."

"I look forward to your full report. The General, over and out."

Ramses lowered the radio from his ear. He felt a twinge of disappointment — to this point, Osborne had been his responsibility and he felt slighted to be yanked off the case midstream. Yet he was in no position to second-guess the General. He pursed his lips as he set the radio back on the desk in front of him and glanced at the mirror again.

He saw his reflection — and behind him a woman, with two hands clutching a large bore revolver pointed straight at his head. He froze and waited for her to speak first.

"Hands in the air," she ordered.

Ramses silently obeyed, as he shot the woman an icy stare through the mirror. She had short brown hair, hidden under the hood of a red sweatshirt. Her features were soft — soft nose, large eyes, thin lips.

"You work for the General?" she asked.

Ramses nodded, as he continued to examine the woman for any identifying marks.

"Who is he?" she asked.

"I don't know," Ramses replied. "I only know him as the General." That much was true — Ramses guessed the General was ex-military, but even that was only an assumption.

"And 'Osborne' — you were talking about John Osborne?" she asked.

"Yes," Ramses said. "You know him?"

"You could say that," the woman replied with a smug grin. "What's his connection to the General?"

Ramses paused. What was this woman after?

"Answer the question," the woman demanded.

"You might say he's the General's strongman," said Ramses — a lie, albeit a plausible one. She couldn't have heard the other side of the radio conversation.

The woman didn't reply for a moment. Ramses noticed she had a small tattoo across her right wrist — something written in a script he couldn't recognize.

"And why is he going to Mallard Island?"

"The General sent him there on business."

"Business?"

"Arms project." Ramses suppressed a smirk.

The woman eyed him warily, tightening her grip around the revolver.

"And what's *your* next move?" she said.

"Me? I just hope to walk away from here alive."

The woman glared at him. Then without another word she stepped back, away from the mirror, and her reflection disappeared from Ramses' view. He heard the front door open then shut. After waiting cautiously for a few moments, Ramses lowered his arms.

*How could she know about the General* and *John Osborne,* he wondered, *and yet be so clueless as to the details?* Thankfully, she'd readily accepted his misdirection, though he wasn't sure he'd made the correct play. The General wanted Osborne alive ... what did that woman want?

*There's nothing I can do now,* Ramses realized. Whatever she had come looking for, he'd just made it John Osborne's problem.

# Chapter 21

*SOME PEOPLE IN this world don't know what do to with themselves,* Aristotle thought. Watching John in Franco's Saloon was like watching a gray wolf try to play with two Yorkshire Terriers. It just couldn't work. Yet she had decided to let him go; to give him a chance.

If indeed he was out causing trouble — and tangled up with the General, no less — that was on *her* conscience now. Her mission was to find the General himself, but that would have to wait. She was off to find out if what that soldier had said about John was true.

Her feet carried her north through the woods, toward Ontario Highway 11. From there she'd head east to Mallard Island. If John was still a free agent, maybe she could swing him to her side. But if he was in league with the General?

Aristotle looked down, glancing at the handcrafted revolver that rested in her holster. Could she best John Osborne in a shootout?

She hoped she wouldn't have to find out.

You have reached the conclusion of *A Stranger North*, but the chronicles are far from over.

In late summer of last year I wrote a short story to bridge the gap between the book you've just finished reading and the next book in the series, *Spear Hunter*.

Formerly an online-exclusive, this story, *Ramses' Thunder*, appears for the first time in print here.

I hope you enjoy it.

*-HJO*

# Ramses' Thunder

IF ONLY he'd had a car.

What was a car?

A car was a vehicle that could transport a person from place to place. A car, faster and stronger than even the most formidable beast of burden, subsisted on a diet of pure gasoline and exhaled thick plumes of gray smoke. The car had been the defining invention of the 20th century, a commodity which had given new meaning to the American dream. A car was a glorious machine that could cover hundreds of miles a day.

A car was also a luxury that Ramses Brushnell had to do without. A mere mortal lacking a motor, Ramses could cover a few dozen miles a day at best.

Ramses was making his way south toward the Restoration Army's central headquarters. He carried only the most essential of a gear: a small pack on his back and a pistol at his side.

Presently, he was passing through the forests of northern Minnesota. During the dog days of summer the forest was like a jungle. While the lush green leaves overhead protected him from the stifling heat of the afternoon sun, those same leaves also trapped moisture and kept it close to the ground, ensuring that Ramses' trek was a humid one. Already sweat had crept into every last thread of his green Restoration Army fatigues. The well-worn uniform would need replacing as soon as he arrived at HQ.

Unfortunately, it would still take days, perhaps even weeks, of walking before Ramses arrived at his destination. If ever he'd wanted a car, it was now. Yet he knew the possibility of finding a car, to speak nothing of gasoline, was effectively zero. The age of machines had ended. Now men lived in a new age, an age of greater freedom but also of greater individual responsibility. For all he'd lost, Ramses still felt this new age was the one he'd been born to live in. It was an age that suited his strengths.

Having no watch, Ramses had resorted to estimating the time according to the position of the sun. When he spotted a rustic farmhouse in the distance that afternoon, however, Ramses didn't need to check the blazing ball above to know that it was the day's hottest hour.

Typically, the sight of a farmhouse barely piqued Ramses' interest. In the years since the Desolation survivors had already picked through most of the abandoned homes, and most of what they'd left behind was either worthless or had long since gone bad. Still, Ramses hoped that with a little luck he might find a few useful supplies inside this house. Bullets and canned goods were of particular interest; most other items weren't worth the weight they'd add to his pack.

As he drew closer, however, he realized that this farmhouse was no ordinary abandoned homestead. Just beyond the house stood a large barn sporting a clean coat of white paint. Beside the barn, in turn, was a fenced-in area where over half a dozen horses roamed.

Ramses eyed the horses enviously. Though any thought of procuring a car was but a foolish dream, a speedy, vigorous horse would be a fair consolation prize. Ramses drew his pistol, holding it with both hands, and cautiously approached the stable. It took only an effortless climb over the shoulder-high fence and he was inside.

Admittedly, Ramses knew little of horses. He wondered if the General had considered adding mounted soldiers to the ranks of the Restoration Army. It seemed a logical idea. Then again, perhaps mounted troops didn't fit within the General's grand vision of the future. A wise man well-versed in the ways of the world, the General surely had his sights set on greater things.

The horses looked healthy and fit to ride. Though the General didn't openly condone theft, he did value expedience. Seeing as he was in a hurry, stealing a horse appeared to be Ramses' best option. All he had to do was mount one without being caught, teach himself how to ride, and then continue on his way — a masterful plan if there ever was one.

Taking care not to cause alarm, Ramses approached one of the horses, a chestnut-colored steed that stood just a hair taller than himself. Was this horse male or female? Did it know how to carry a rider? And how did one go about riding a horse, anyhow? Ramses was unsure how to ascertain the answers to these questions, and, unfortunately, time wasn't on his side. Hopefully trial and error would teach him quickly.

"Hello there, friend!"

The voice came from the direction of the farmhouse. Fast as an enraged mother bear, Ramses spun toward the voice and extended his pistol arm. His pistol's sights landed on a man standing near the farmhouse, about twenty yards out.

"Don't move," Ramses ordered. "Keep your hands where I can see them."

"I have no intention of moving, my friend." The man lifted his hands above his head. He had dark, brownish-red skin and long black hair streaked with gray, tied in a ponytail that ran down his back. He wore a simple white button-up shirt and navy blue jeans. His deep eyes glimmered as though he had not a care in the world — an impressive feat, considering he had a pistol pointed in his face.

"May I ask your name?" the man asked.

Ramses glowered in reply. Recently, he'd been reading *Taking the Power Back,* a book about negotiation penned by Howard Armstrong Steel. Steel's 9th Law was 'Speak only when necessary,' and now wasn't the time to speak. Slowly, Ramses paced closer. Though he was good with a pistol, closing the distance between him and his target would give him more room for error.

"Not one beholden to words, it seems," the pony-tailed man said. "Well then, take what you will and be gone. I won't try to stop you."

Ramses lips curled into a smug grin. "You say that only because you know you can't stop me."

"That very well may be true," the man admitted. "However, I sense there are obstacles besides myself that stand between you and what you wish to accomplish."

Ramses came to a halt about ten yards from the man. He kept his target's face squarely in his pistol's sights.

"If you're trying to convince me you have backup, you're doing a poor job," Ramses mocked.

The man offered a hint of a shrug, careful to keep his movement subdued. "I saw you examining my horses. Your confounded expression betrayed your inexperience. I could see that you don't know the difference between a foal and a mare, much less how to ride a horse. Trying to commandeer one and hightail out of here would only add to your troubles. You must learn how to ride, first."

Ramses furrowed his brow. The pony-tailed man was right, of course. Ramses had grown up working with tvapas — hardy, moose-like creatures bred to thrive even in the coldest of Minnesota winters — and horses were completely foreign to him. Still, for all his ignorance, he was certain that riding a horse would be exponentially faster than trekking by foot. Though learning to ride would require a few days, afterward he would be able to regain any time lost.

"Are you offering to teach me how to ride?" Ramses said dismissively, as to suggest the offer was below him — an unnecessary kindness.

"Don't get ahead of yourself, my friend," the man said. "Let us step inside to chat over a cup of tea. We shall see where the conversation takes us. However, first you must holster your weapon."

"I'm afraid that's not an option," Ramses said, his fingers tightening around the pistol.

"Do as you wish. Should you change your mind, I shall be waiting right here."

Careful to keep an eye on the man, Ramses proceeded back to the horse he'd been examining earlier. He put his free hand high on the horse's back, near its spine.

How did one mount a horse? It would take both hands, he realized. Warily, Ramses glanced at the pony-tailed man. The man hadn't moved, save to lower his arms. It didn't appear he had a weapon. Confident he wouldn't be relinquishing the upper hand, Ramses ate his words and slid his pistol into its holster.

With both hands free, Ramses reached again for horse's upper side and tried to hoist himself up. As soon as he put pressure on the horse's back, the horse whinnied and paced forward a few steps. The movement, though not aggressive, was enough for the horse to shake free of Ramses' grasp and send him falling flat on his backside.

Ramses let out a sigh of discontent. This obviously wasn't going to work. After picking himself up and brushing the dirt from his pants, he strode towards the man, avoiding eye contact. As it so happened, *Taking the Power Back* had given him perfect advice for just this situation.

*Steel's 16th Law: 'Never make needless eye contact with an inferior.'*

"I accept your offer," Ramses stated, holding his nose high as he looked off into the distance. "Let's step into your hovel and have some of your so-called tea." He continued walking forward, not waiting for the man.

"You strut as though you own this place," the man called out from behind.

Ramses stepped up to the front door of the farmhouse. "Get used to it. Not even this backwoods shack is beyond the General's reach."

"Who is the General?" the man asked.

"You will find out soon enough," Ramses replied as he shoved the door open and let himself inside.

\* \* \*

Ramses sat at a table in the farmhouse's kitchen, admiring the interior. The building was in better condition than he'd expected. The windows were spotless, the tablecloth had nary a stain, and the hardwood chairs didn't creak under his weight. This pony-tailed recluse had done an surprisingly admirable job of maintaining the home.

The man stood over a wood-fired stove, brewing tea. Steam from the kettle sent subtle notes of pine drifting through the kitchen. The scene reminded Ramses of his youth. These days, tea was a luxury for which he had little time.

Ramses still didn't know the man's name. Neither of them had spoken a word since stepping inside, and Ramses refused to be the one who broke the silence.

*Steel's 8th Law: 'Always make the other man speak first.'*

The man poured the hot brew into two fine ceramic teacups. After setting one in front of Ramses, he took a seat at the table.

"Forgive me for not having ice. I know chilled tea would be preferable in this heat," the man said, smiling apologetically.

Ramses didn't reply. With one hand, he lifted the teacup to his lips and took a sip. Although the brew's immediate flavor was rather mild, it left a bitter aftertaste lingering on the back of his tongue.

"Can you taste the poison?" the man asked cheerily. "I did my best to mask it."

*Desolation!* Cringing with revulsion, Ramses spat the drink from his mouth. Had he swallowed a lethal dose? He dropped to his knees and shoved his fingers down his throat, trying to coax himself to vomit.

How had he fallen for such a simple ruse? He'd forgotten to abide by Steel's 17th Law: *'Never trust a product the salesman himself doesn't use.'*

"A very literal fellow, I see." The man stood over Ramses. He offered his hand. "That, my friend, was what I call a joke."

*A joke?* It was a joke as unwelcome as a hive of yellow jackets. Tacitly rejecting the man's helping hand, Ramses returned to his feet by his own power.

"Pride — a time-honored killer of men," the man said, reclaiming his seat.

Ramses gave the man the evil eye before also retaking his seat at the table. What game was this pony-tailed hermit playing?

The man took a sip of his tea. "I brew this tea from pine needles and wild rice. It is a favorite of mine." He set his cup back on the table. "My name is Gerard. And you?"

"Ramses."

Waiting to speak hadn't worked as Ramses had intended. He'd made a fool of himself instead. *Brilliant. Absolutely brilliant.*

"It is a pleasure, Ramses. Not often do I get visitors. May I ask what brings you to these parts?"

"You may ask anything you like," Ramses said flippantly. Whether he would offer answers or not was another matter.

"How about you start by telling —"

"How about we start with your life story, instead," Ramses countered. "How long have you been living here?"

*Steel's 30th Law: 'Cut them off when they least expect it.'*

"Me?" Gerard uttered, scratching his chin. "Oh, about a year or so."

"And before that?" Ramses stared across the table, digging into Gerard with his eyes.

"Before that? I owned a bakery in Duluth until the Desolation struck, at which point I abandoned the business for obvious reasons. I lost my family during that time, as well." He took a moment to solemnly cast his eyes toward the floor, before lifting his head back up and continuing. "And now I am here. What else is there to know?"

"That leaves about eight years unaccounted for."

A grin formed on the outer corners of Gerard's lips. "Are you planning to write my biography?"

"A preposterous idea," Ramses snickered.

The conversation died there, and neither man moved to revive it. The hollow thumps of a woodpecker knocking on a tree outside reverberated into the kitchen.

Ramses took another sip of his tea, reflecting upon his folly. Had the concoction he was drinking actually contained poison, he surely would've tasted it. He decided that if he ever found himself in a similar situation, he would trust his tongue.

The tea had become lukewarm when Gerald again spoke.

"The truth is, it embarrasses me to admit what happened during those eight years. I spent the first few in Duluth, until eventually I was roped into joining the Great Society of the Redemption."

"The Great Society of the Redemption?" Even the name reeked of pretense.

"You've not heard of it?" Gerard asked, touching his tea cup to his lips.

"No," Ramses replied smugly.

"A cult of sorts, the Great Society of the Redemption is led by a charismatic chap named Mathias West. Reverend West claims that the Desolation was punishment for man's sins, and that it is our responsibility as survivors to build a new and better world."

"A belief ridiculous to its very core," Ramses scoffed. "How could you fall for such a ploy?"

"It's easier than you might imagine." Gerard wrapped his hands around his teacup. "Reverend West found me at a dark time in my life and offered his leadership. I was eager to follow his guidance and seek redemption."

"And what convinced you to leave?" Ramses asked, gazing at his hands absentmindedly. His fingernails were long overdue for a trim.

*Steel's 12th Law: 'Show complete disinterest.'*

"I grew disillusioned with his teachings," Gerard said, shaking his head. "I am not a great thinker by any means, but even I could see the contradictions in Reverend West's theology. Unfortunately, when we want to believe, we are all too willing to overlook such things."

Ramses rolled his eyes. "Speak for yourself."

"Are you certain that you are above such influence?" Gerard squinted curiously at Ramses.

"Absolutely."

"This man you mentioned, the General, is not in any way similar to Reverend West?"

Gerard's question took Ramses by surprise, like a warning shot across his nose. He clutched his thighs and leaned forward in his chair.

"The General is a great man," he proclaimed. "How dare you compare him to a lowly charlatan such as this Mathew East!"

"Mathias West," Gerard corrected.

"What difference does it make?" Ramses said, throwing his hands above his head.

Gerard shrugged. "Does the General have a plan? A vision, perhaps?"

"Of course!" Ramses pounded his fist on the table. "The General plans to bring civilization back to Minnesota. No longer will you and I be stuck living in backwoods shacks like this hovel you call home. A new age will dawn, and we shall return to the comforts and conveniences of the life we once knew."

"Sounds familiar." Gerard idly drummed his fingers on the table. "The most impressive thing is that this General didn't even need to resort to religious overtones to hook you."

"What are you babbling about?" Ramses spat out.

"That is for you to figure out, my friend. In the meantime, why don't you get some rest? You will need to be in peak condition if you wish to learn how to ride," Gerard said, rising from his seat and making for the door out of the kitchen.

"Really?" Ramses asked, narrowing his eyes with suspicion. "You'll teach me how to ride a horse?"

"I'll consider it. In the meantime, I shall prepare the guest room and a change of clothes for you." Gerard smiled. "The vest and fatigues you wear have seen better days."

* * *

After a much-needed night of rest, the next morning Ramses donned the collared white shirt and pair of jeans that Gerard had lent him and went downstairs for breakfast. He and Gerard indulged in a hearty breakfast of wild game and sweet potatoes, and then set out to talk horses.

Using the chestnut horse Ramses had tried to mount the day before — a stallion named Thunder, as it turned out — Gerard demonstrated how to groom, saddle, and bridle a horse. Seemingly having forgotten Ramses' threats the day prior, Gerard served as an eager teacher, and by lunchtime

Ramses had learned much. Though he hadn't tried to mount the horse again, Ramses now understood how foolhardy he'd been to think he could simply hop on a horse and ride away.

The late-summer sun was bearing down from directly above when Gerard went inside to fetch a heaping plate of deer jerky for the noon meal. He set the dish on an oak picnic table beside the farmhouse and invited Ramses to sit and help himself. Ramses obliged, snatching a palm sized piece of the tough, chewy meat and tearing into it with his canines.

*Steel's 33rd Law: 'Show your teeth.'*

Gerard sat on the picnic bench opposite Ramses, gnawing at a chunk of jerky before swallowing it.

"So, why did you want to ride off with Thunder?" he asked, sounding genuinely interested rather than accusatory.

"Because a horse can run faster than I can," Ramses said, smirking at his clever non-answer. He'd known an interrogation was inevitable. Fortunately, he'd already prepared vague answers to the questions he expected Gerard to ask. Howard Armstrong Steel would be proud. Steel's 1st Law was 'Be prepared.'

Gerard grabbed another piece of jerky and bit off a mouthful. "What is the hurry?"

"I'm going somewhere and I need to arrive as soon as possible," Ramses said

"I see that. But why must you rush? It seems that you have everything you need right here: food, shelter, and decent company. What else could a man want for?"

"Purpose," Ramses declared. "You lack purpose."

"My purpose is to tend my horses, keep my property tidy, and take care of myself. Those three responsibilities provide me purpose enough to keep my soul content."

Ramses picked up a second piece of jerky. He admired its texture before stuffing the whole chunk into his mouth. "You're like a hamster spinning a wheel. You call that purpose?"

Gerard shrugged. "It is enough."

"Have you no ambition?" Ramses said, chomping at the jerky.

"My ambition is to live a long and prosperous life. Nothing more."

Ramses shook his head. "You sound just like the fools I left behind in my old village."

"And where might your old village be?" Gerard asked.

"I've already said too much," Ramses muttered, gazing off into the distance. These days, he never mentioned the name of his village. To associate himself with such a backwater hamlet was a disservice to his own burgeoning reputation.

Gerard scratched his chin. "Duluth?"

Ramses gave a derisive laugh.

"I suppose not," Gerard said. "How about International Falls?"

Ramses said nothing, confident that Gerard would never guess correctly. His village wasn't even on the map.

"Toronto?" Gerard tried again.

"Give it up," Ramses urged.

"Or perhaps you're from Frontier View?"

Ramses eye's swung back to Gerard's face. He gave the man an intense stare. How had this solitary recluse guessed his hometown?

"Frontier View, huh? Not a bad place. I visited once," Gerard said casually.

"You did?" Ramses raised an eyebrow. Perhaps Gerard had more depth than his simple appearance and lifestyle suggested. On the other hand, Frontier View wasn't *that* far from Gerard's backwoods hovel. Ramses shouldn't have been so surprised that the man had once been there.

"Well, strictly speaking, 'visited' might not be the best word." Gerard grinned. "But yes, I've been there before."

"When? And why?" Ramses asked. Frontier View rarely saw travelers, and thus the arrival of an outsider was always a minor event, one Ramses felt he would have remembered. Was it possible he'd simply forgotten Gerard? Or perhaps Gerard's visit had come within the past year, after Ramses' departure from the village.

"That, my friend, is a story for another day," Gerard said with a sly grin.

Ramses fumed as the two men finished their meal in silence.

That afternoon, Gerard demonstrated how to properly mount a horse and adjust the stirrups. He then let Ramses try. After Ramses mounted the animal successfully, Gerard instructed him in the basics of commanding the horse. To ask the horse to walk, Ramses gently squeezed with both legs. To stop, he pulled back on the horse's reins. After becoming comfortable with starting and stopping, he then learned how to guide the horse left and right by tugging the reins in the desired direction and gently nudging the horse with the opposite leg. By the time the evening sun threatened to disappear behind the trees, he felt comfortable riding the horse around the stable.

"That's all for today," Gerard said. "Let's take him in for the night and have dinner."

Ramses carefully dismounted the horse, using a stirrup for balance. He handed the reins to Gerard.

"Thunder is a name fit for a war horse. How did he get it?" he asked.

"I'm glad you asked," Gerard said, brushing a fallen strand of black hair from his white shirt. "I met Thunder one stormy night last year. I was outside, trying to shoo the last of my horses into the barn — no easy task when you can hardly see your own feet in front of you.

"Just as I had finished rounding up the horses and was ready to head inside to escape the heavy downpour, I heard something clopping through the puddles. I shined my lamp into the distance, but it was no use. I could barely see my hands, much less whatever was out there.

"Then, a huge bolt of lightning forked across the sky, revealing the source of the noise — a horse running madly through the stormy night. When lightning flashed again, it became clear that the horse had seen me as well, because he had changed course and was now galloping toward me. The following moment, as thunder rumbled through the air, the horse emerged from the darkness, appearing inside the cone of light cast from my lamp.

"Immediately, I could tell that he was friendly. He had no qualms about letting me coral him into my barn. Hard rain pelted the roof and thunder shook the earth as I helped him settle in for the night, and from that day on his name was Thunder."

"He was already domesticated when he came to you?" Ramses asked.

"Someone else had already broken Thunder, yes. I treated him with care and he quickly came to trust me as well."

"And his owner never came looking for him?"

"No, conveniently enough."

Gerard led Thunder into the barn. After ensuring all of the horses had plenty of hay and water, the two men went inside to prepare dinner. Ramses sat at the kitchen table while Gerard stood at the counter, cutting carrots and potatoes. A pot of water slowly warmed toward a simmer on the stove top.

"How do you manage on your own?" Ramses asked, legitimately curious. When he'd left Frontier View the year before, he'd originally intended to strike out on his own. The prospect of living alone turned out to be more daunting than he'd imagined, however, and when Ramses heard the General's overtures, he'd decided they were too full of promise to ignore.

"It requires a good measure of faith," Gerard said wistfully.

"Faith?" Ramses said, cocking his head. "I thought you'd left your faith behind."

"There are many kinds of faith," Gerard explained. "My faith in the teachings of Mathias West was decidedly misplaced. I now instead place my faith in the land."

"In the land?" Ramses asked skeptically.

"I plant seeds, set traps, and tend to my farm. I trust that if I put in my fair share of effort, the land will provide for me. Thus far it has kept its end of the bargain without fail."

"And you call that faith?"

"When I slave over my vegetable garden in the first week of spring, or set snares in the cold of winter, I cannot be sure of what rewards I will reap. Not all of my seeds grow into edible crops, nor do all of my traps catch game. However, I trust that my efforts will yield enough for me to get by. I consider this to be a form of faith."

"And what if the land fails you?" Ramses said, raising his brow.

"Then I will know my faith was misplaced," Gerard said, using his knife to guide the freshly cut vegetables from his cutting board into the stew pot.

"But why not strive for more? Not only to survive, but to thrive?"

"Last time our species tried to thrive, as you say, we did so by bending nature to our will. Our hubris led to depleted aquifers, arid fields, and unbearably hot summers, a result which made it quite clear that man, despite his inclinations to believe otherwise, cannot conquer nature. The world can be contorted to mankind's will for a time, yes, but eventually the pendulum must swing back the other way."

Ramses didn't reply. The logic of Gerard's response relied upon accepting the concept of balance. Was every inch of darkness in the universe was offset by an equal patch of light? To this question Ramses had no answer. Still, he had no intentions of leaving his future to the whims of the land. The General planned to create a stronger and more abundant world for men. Certainly the General's path was the best, both in the short and long-term.

The stew simmered on the stove. When it was finished, Ramses and Gerard dined under the fading light of day.

* * *

Ramses awoke at dawn the next morning to the plaintive cooing of a mourning dove. He lay lazily in bed, staring at the guest room's hardwood ceiling. Admittedly, the accommodations were the best he'd enjoyed in months. In addition to the soft bed, the room had a masterfully crafted desk with a matching chair and an oak bookshelf stacked full of old paperback novels.

Gerard's home was comfortable — more comfortable than Ramses liked. He rose from bed, slipped into the shirt and jeans Gerard had lent him, and went downstairs. Gerard was standing over the kitchen stove, putting the finishing touches on a breakfast of scrambled eggs and bacon.

"Morning, my friend," Gerard greeted.

Ramses silently arranged two plates and sets of utensils at the table before taking a seat. Gerard carried his frying pan over and distributed the heavy, protein rich meal onto the plates. He then set the pan on a cooking mitt in the center of the table and sat opposite Ramses.

"Dig in," Gerard offered. "This may be your last breakfast here."

"Oh?" Ramses uttered, intrigued.

"While you're not a professional rider yet, you have learned enough to get to where you're going." Gerard smiled easily. "Wherever that may be."

*Wherever that may be?* Clearly Gerard was trying to surreptitiously root out the location of Restoration Army HQ. Surely he didn't think Ramses would divulge the secret so easily?

"How much more is there for me to learn?"

"Today we shall go over how to trot. That should be enough. Push the horse any faster and you risk wearing him out before you arrive. Beyond that, as long as you remember to properly groom and care for the horse, you should be fine."

Ramses quietly shoveled a forkful of egg into his mouth. The whinny of a horse filtered in through the open window.

"Mind if I ask you a question?" Gerard asked, setting his fork on his plate.

Ramses eyed Gerard, before returning to his meal. There was no point in responding. He knew Gerard would ask regardless of his answer.

*Steel's 22nd Law: 'Treat frivolous questions with contempt.'*

"Why did you leave Frontier View?" Gerard asked.

Ramses contemplated a moment, continuing to eat, before answering, "Frontier View is a stifling place. I grew tired of answering to the elders there."

"Yet now you answer to another boss."

"The circumstances are completely different," Ramses said.

"The new boss is same as the old boss," Gerard quipped. "That is how The Who put it, roughly speaking."

"Who?" Ramses asked, unsure if he was being toyed with again or not.

"The Who," Gerard replied, straight-faced.

Ramses shot Gerard a dirty look. He then stabbed his fork into a slab of bacon, shoved it into his mouth, and viciously ground it into mush between his canines and molars.

"Sorry," Gerard apologized. "I get a little carried away with my rock n' roll allusions. What I am trying to say is that while your new life offers the illusion of freedom, you are still under someone's thumb."

"I suppose that's true," Ramses replied, "but in this case it's by choice."

"A valid distinction." Gerard nodded, rubbing his chin. With a shrug, he took his fork and continued to work at his food.

After breakfast, the two men went outside to work with Thunder. As promised, Gerard showed Ramses how to trot. Ramses soon learned that there were two methods of trotting: the slow trot and the rising trot.

Riding the horse at a slow trot was little different than riding it at a walk, and Ramses quickly mastered the technique. The rising trot, on the other hand, was slightly more difficult. Ramses had to rise up and sit down in his saddle in time with the horse's gait, and it took a few hours of practice for him to grow comfortable with the motion. By the time he dismounted for a break, Ramses' white shirt was drenched with sticky sweat.

Ramses grimaced as Gerard gave him a hearty pat on the shoulder. Even the gentlest touch aggravated his sweaty skin.

"I believe you are ready, my friend" Gerard said.

"I am?" Ramses said, his surprise masked by exhaustion.

"Pack your things while I make lunch. You will set off with Thunder this afternoon."

Ramses nodded in acknowledgment and proceeded to the guest room. He had little to pack. As he stuffed the camping gear and basic cookware he'd procured from a Restoration Army outpost into his bag, he heard Gerard's approaching footsteps.

Ramses stopped packing and stood, stepping away from the bag.

*Steel's 7th Law: 'Never let them see what you're doing.'*

"Do you like to read?" Gerard asked from the doorway.

"Occasionally," Ramses offered.

Gerard leaned against the door frame, crossing his arms. "You are free to borrow a book or two from the bookshelf. I have more books than I will ever be able read." After momentarily admiring his book collection, Gerard retreated to the hallway. He glanced back at Ramses and added, "Lunch will be ready in five minutes. Don't be late."

Ramses walked to the bookshelf and scanned the titles. Gerard had a diverse library, ranging from classic literature to history books to guides about Minnesota plant life.

That's when Ramses saw it. There, hidden on the lowest shelf, was a copy of *Taking the Power Back* by Howard Armstrong Steel.

No wonder none of Ramses negotiation techniques worked as expected! In Gerard, he faced an adversary trained in the very laws he was employing. The pony-tailed recluse was a worthy opponent, indeed.

Overcome with a sense of relief now that he understood that Gerard, too, was a master of Steel's laws, Ramses looked again to the bookshelf and deliberated which titles to take. Eventually, he settled on two Jack London novels, *White Fang* and *The Call of the Wild,* adding them to his pack before returning downstairs to the kitchen.

For lunch, Ramses and Gerard dined on pan-seared pork chops and sweet potato hash browns cooked in the leftover pork fat. Ramses savored the delicious food, knowing it might be the last home-cooked meal he'd enjoy for a long time. Though the kitchen at Restoration Army HQ steadfastly ensured that all the General's men were fed, it wasn't known for its world-class cuisine.

When they finished eating, Ramses and Gerard returned outside to prepare Thunder for the journey ahead.

Ramses ran a hand down Thunder's mane. "You're really going to let me take him?" he asked, suspiciously.

"Thunder came to me much the same way you did, my friend," Gerard said. "He is not mine to keep or give away. If he wishes to join you on your journey, it is not my place to stop him."

"I see," Ramses said, scratching Thunder behind the ear.

"You and Thunder are welcome to return anytime. My door is always open, and you may remain here as long as you wish."

"Surely you aren't expecting me to stay," Ramses said flatly. "You live well here, I'll admit, but I aspire to do more than simply live well."

"I expect nothing, and I take only that which I am given. It is always enough," Gerard said.

Ramses smirked wryly. Though he disagreed with the principles by which Gerard lived, he'd developed an odd respect for the man. Using the skills Gerard had taught him, he set a foot in Thunder's stirrup and hoisted himself into the saddle.

"This is farewell," he declared.

"You have not yet told me where it is you're hurrying off to," Gerard said.

Ramses stared off into the nearly endless wilderness that surrounded the farmhouse. Was there any harm in sharing his destination?

*Steel's 40th Law: 'Let them think they've won.'*

"Your persistence is admirable," Ramses finally said. "I'm going to Minneapolis."

"Minneapolis is quite a ways yet. You can push Thunder a bit, but make sure to pace him. The journey should take five or six days," Gerard said, nodding contemplatively. "Thunder is yours now. I trust you will treat him well."

"Thanks for the advice," Ramses replied. He paused for a moment, before adding, "I respect a man who studies the 40 Laws of Steel."

"The what?" Gerard asked, evidently perplexed.

"I saw *Taking the Power Back* on your bookshelf. I presume you've read it?" Ramses asked.

"Oh, that? Many of those books were already here when I moved in. Perhaps one day I shall read the book of which you speak."

"I see ..." Ramses trailed off.

"Have a safe journey," Gerard said. "You will not be soon forgotten." With a smile and a wave, he turned to walk away, stepping into his farmhouse and closing the door without looking back.

Ramses watched in wonderment. Had Gerard really not read the Laws of Steel? Or, by denying that he'd studied the book, was he implementing Steel's Laws with a degree of expertise that even Ramses himself couldn't match?

For better or for worse, the journey ahead would offer ample time to ponder the encounter. Ramses took Thunder's reins and gently squeezed the horse's sides, urging the horse forward.

No longer did he need a car, for Ramses had found his Thunder.

## About The Author

Henry J. Olsen grew up as a quiet kid in a small Wisconsin town. Now he travels the world and writes tales of adventure.

As of this writing he eats, sleeps, and writes in Kaohsiung, Taiwan.

Follow him via his blog:
http://simplyunbound.com

**Also by Henry J. Olsen**

<u>The Northland Chronicles</u>
*Spear Hunter*
*Desolation's Wake* (Coming in 2015)

<u>Other Works</u>
*Bullies*

*See you on Mallard Island.*

www.ingramcontent.com/pod-product-compliance
Lightning Source LLC
Chambersburg PA
CBHW070938130626
46555CB00001B/491